W9-BCP-310

ON THE EDGE

ALSO BY ALLISON VAN DIEPEN

Street Pharm

Snitch

Takedown

THE
EDGE

ALLISON VAN
DIEPEN

HARPER TEEN

An Imprint of HarperCollinsPublishers

HarperTeen is an imprint of HarperCollins Publishers.

On the Edge
Copyright © 2014 by Allison van Diepen
All rights reserved. Printed in the United States of America.
No part of this book may be used or reproduced in any manner whatsoever without written permission except in the case of brief quotations embodied in critical articles and reviews.
For information address HarperCollins Children's Books, a division of HarperCollins Publishers, 195 Broadway, New York, NY 10007.
www.epicreads.com

Library of Congress Cataloging-in-Publication Data
Van Diepen, Allison.
    On the edge / Allison van Diepen. — First edition.
        pages   cm
    Summary: "When Maddie Diaz witnesses the murder of a homeless man by members of a gang, she tells the cops what she saw without thinking about the repercussions of snitching, but a mysterious guy named Lobo comes to her defense and is determined to take down the gang and protect her"— Provided by publisher.
    ISBN 978-0-06-230344-8 (hardback)
    [1. Witnesses—Fiction.   2. Gangs—Fiction.   3. Hispanic Americans—Fiction.]
I. Title.
PZ7.V28526On   2014   2014022032
[Fic]—dc23   CIP
                                                            AC

Typography by Ellice M. Lee
14 15 16 17 18 LP/RRDH 10 9 8 7 6 5 4 3 2 1
❖
First Edition

For Jeremy

THE PRIZE

"HOW ARE WE CELEBRATING TONIGHT?" My best friend, Isadora, grabbed me in a bear hug from behind.

I laughed, then pried her off me. "I'm sure you can come up with something. I work till nine."

It was so unreal. I'd been hoping to get into Florida State for as long as I could remember. But the scholarship was a surprise. My tuition was covered for *four whole years*. Sure, I'd still have to work my butt off for living expenses and books, but I had no complaints.

Hasta luego, *Miami. Sorry, I won't miss you.*

I couldn't wait to tell Mom. She'd already left for work when the admissions package arrived, and I'd been dying to text her with the news. But then I wouldn't get to see the look on her face when I told her. And I couldn't miss that.

"Come to my place after work. We'll party with the girls. I'm so proud of you!" Iz kissed my cheek, which would now be smeared with her trademark bright red lipstick.

"It's so last minute, Iz. Abby and Carmen might already have plans."

"They're in. I texted them this morning. I'm gonna make a special drink for tonight. I'm calling it the Maddie Diaz Margarita."

I grinned. "What's gonna be in it?"

"A *ton* of tequila."

Her phone rang. She wrenched it out of the pocket of her tight designer jeans. "Rob, I told you not to call me at school." She groaned. "I said I had to cancel tonight. I don't care how much you paid for the seats. My girl got a scholarship!"

I cringed. Iz was an awesome best friend but a terrible girlfriend. Every guy she dated thought he'd struck gold at first, since she looked like a young Eva Longoria. Fast-forward a few weeks, and they'd escape with whatever self-respect they had left. Her latest guy, Rob, had hung on for five months—a record for Iz.

She shoved the phone into her pocket. "What an ass. I wonder why I bother, you know? Now, about tonight, we'll see you at nine fifteen?"

"Ten. I wanna go home and shower first so I don't reek of French fries."

"Good point. Make sure you look extra yummy, okay? I'm inviting some guys to chill with us later on."

Iz's goal in life was to get me a boyfriend. She always complained that I was too closed off to guys, too aloof, but I knew that wasn't the problem. The problem was that none of the guys she tried to hook me up with did anything for me. They were too boring, too blah. They all talked the same shit, smoked the same shit, and rooted for the same sports teams. I wanted a guy who was more . . . something, I just didn't know what.

Maybe I'd find him at Florida State.

As we left the school, we snapped on our knockoff sunglasses. It was only March, but the heat was *hot*. When the city bus pulled up, we packed on with a boatload of other students. I didn't know which was worse: bumping up against sticky skin, or trying not to breathe the stale, sweaty air. I could feel my straightened hair curling up.

"Have you decided about next year?" I asked Iz mid–bus ride. So far, today had been all about my news, and I didn't want her to think that her plans were less important. Iz had a gift for the *artes decorativas*. She could look at any room and see a million possibilities for awesomeness. If I looked at the same space, I would see, well, a room.

"I'm thinking interior design at Miami Dade. My first job will be to decorate *your* dorm room." She fanned herself with her long red fingernails. "You'll come back and see us, right?"

"Of course I'll be back." But the truth was, I couldn't wait to put some distance between me and Miami.

When I got in the door, I dropped my knapsack and cursed. The landlord had promised to fix the air-conditioning today, damn it. Poor Dex. He'd been lying directly under the ceiling fan, but bounced to life when he heard the door.

I opened some windows, then grabbed an iced tea from the fridge and took Dex to the backyard. It was littered with the junk Boyd had left behind: the rusty boat he'd been working on, a Ranger ATV, half-broken patio furniture. Mom didn't want to contact him again to pick up the stuff, since any communication brought on a bunch of nasty voice mails. The divorce would be final soon, thank God.

I threw a ball, and Dex galloped after it. He was the one good thing Boyd had brought into their marriage, and the only good thing he'd left behind.

When Boyd first introduced Dex into our home, I was terrified. Mom had had the nerve to say, "But you always wanted a dog, Maddie."

Yeah, a puppy. Not a hundred pounds of German shepherd.

Home hadn't felt like home anymore. Not with this big,

unpleasant guy and his bloodthirsty dog.

Boyd had kept Dex in the kitchen, closed off by a gate, or tied up in the backyard. It was a shitty life—even I recognized it. I didn't dare go into the kitchen by myself, no matter how hungry I was.

Whenever Boyd wasn't home, I started throwing Dex doggie treats over the gate—a peace offering, so he wouldn't hate me. It worked. Dex would light up, wagging his tail and bouncing around. When I'd go back upstairs, he'd start whining.

Eventually I felt so bad for him that I started letting him out of his kitchen prison, and even taking him for walks. One afternoon when it was just us, I went to my room to take a nap, and woke to find Dex curled up at the foot of my bed.

And that was that.

After playing with Dex for a while, I brought him in while I got dressed for work. I looked at myself in the mirror and frowned. Although I rocked the McDonald's uniform the best I could, my chest was lost in the blouse, and the pants stretched too tight on my hips. At least my friend Abby, a part-time sub jammer, got to wear her own jeans with her Quiznos shirt.

It took ten minutes to walk to work. The early dinner rush had already started, so I grabbed an apron and got going, cooking burgers and dunking fries. Since I'd stuck it out here for two whole years, I was a senior employee and had my pick of jobs. I'd chosen to work in the back. My whole neighborhood ate here, and I didn't want to wait on people I knew.

"Big Mac without cheese," Penny, a single mom, said into the mike.

"Got it," I said, dropping the patties on the griddle.

"Burger biatch Maddie Diaz in da house," came a voice over the speaker.

It was Manny, of course.

"You got an order for me or what?" I called back.

He stuck his head around the corner and winked at me. "Oh, I got something for ya, mamacita."

I rolled my eyes. No matter what raunchiness came out of his mouth, it was never offensive. It was just Manny. "Sorry, I don't eat stale sausage."

He cackled and turned back to his customers.

Manny was twenty-three and had ex-con written all over him—literally. The gang tattoos that covered his arms and chest told the story. But he had turned himself around, or so he said. It wasn't hard to tell that he was into me, since he propositioned me every other week. Although he was cute, with his goatee and crooked smile, he wasn't my type. I might not know exactly what my type was, but he wasn't it.

My shift flew by quicker than usual. After the dinner rush, I took my break and had a salad (I was being good) and a chocolate shake (well, not so good). Then there was some drama when a loudmouthed mom threw her cold fries at Penny the cashier, and Manny had to march her ass out of the place. But even that didn't bug me. I kept thinking of the acceptance letter, the scholarship, and the future so big and bright.

At nine o'clock, I gave up my corner of the kitchen to Anson, a full-timer who'd been working the register.

"Where you taking me tonight?" Manny asked, a mockery of suave. "Don't forget, I'm off at midnight."

"Sorry, Manny. I'm seeing the girls tonight." I thought it was better not to mention what we were celebrating. I doubted Manny had finished high school—gangbangers rarely did. "My friend's playing mixologist at her house."

"What friend? Isa-dora the Explorer?"

"Don't *ever* let her hear you say that."

"I won't. That girl has the *diablo* in her." He shuddered. "Every guy around here knows it."

I grinned. "And yet you all still line up like lambs to the slaughter."

"Not me." His eyes were oddly serious. I could tell he was thinking, *She's not the one I want.* "I'm on break. Let me walk you home."

"Thanks, I'm good. I'll see you tomorrow." I felt a twinge of regret. Manny was a nice guy, but I just couldn't see it happening.

I left McDonald's behind, hurrying toward home. I

couldn't wait to degrease in the shower, put on the cami dress and shoes I'd scored on sale last weekend, and party with my friends.

And tell my mom the big news.

I found her in the backyard, smoking a cigarette and nursing a Diet Coke. She'd started smoking again when Boyd had moved in, after having quit for ten years. Now that he was gone, she'd at least agreed to smoke outside.

"I got this today." I handed her the acceptance letter, my face not giving anything away.

She butted out her cigarette and read it. "Scholarship! Oh my God, Maddie!" She jumped off the lawn chair. "Oh my God!"

Mom caught me in a hug, laughing and crying at the same time. *This* Mom, this exuberant Mom, was the one I'd always loved. The mom before Dad died. My happiness was her happiness. Maybe this good news would help piece us together again.

Maybe.

My eyes welled up. For three years, Mom had chosen Boyd over me. His needs, his rules, his comfort. Sometimes I wondered if she still resented me for never giving him a chance. But how could I? I knew right away what it took her so long to figure out: that he was an asshole. It was obvious from the way he'd kicked Dex around.

Screw it. Mom was back, and that was all that mattered.

"Let's celebrate, Madeleina! Come, I'll make us some taquitos."

"Sorry, Mom. Iz is having a little party for me."

A flash of disappointment crossed her face. Was it so surprising? I'd been spending most of my free time at Iz's place for years. Mom never used to complain about it. But now that Boyd was gone, she wanted more from me.

"All right." Mom mustered up a smile. "Then I'll help you get ready."

FLAME

"LET'S GET THIS PARTY STARTED!" The second I walked in the door, Iz shoved a lime green margarita into my hand.

Abby and Carmen pushed past her to give me hugs. The music was pumped up. Iz's mom and stepdad manned a food truck in South Beach—Friday and Saturday nights were prime time for them.

And for us.

Iz's house had the same layout as mine, but couldn't be more different. Her personality was splashed all over the walls—bright reds, blues, and yellows, like you'd find in a Mexican restaurant. The living and dining rooms were decorated with flea market finds, including a hurricane lamp, artwork in wicker frames, a driftwood coffee table, and fresh flowers stuffed into mason jars. Iz called it "shabby beach chic." I had no doubt that with her help, I'd have the coolest dorm room at Florida State.

"Drink up, girl," Iz said. "We got some guys coming later."

I sipped the margarita and winced. "Holy, that's strong."

"It has to be. You're one margarita behind the rest of us."

We plunked down on the couches and caught up on our week. Iz and I went to a different school from Abby and Carmen. Back in junior high, Iz and I had won spaces, by lottery, to William Morgan Preparatory Academy—a better school in a better neighborhood. A school where the (mostly white) students were actually expected to go to college. A school where I'd gained social acceptance because one of the "in" crowd had said I looked like Demi Lovato.

Luckily, two different schools meant double the drama to rehash every week.

"Which guys are coming tonight?" Carmen asked, stirring the umbrella in her margarita. Short and Kardashian curvy, Carmen could attract a guy's attention, but didn't have the confidence to back it up.

"Not Eric," Iz said bluntly. "Sorry, hon."

"You should give up on that one," Abby said. She was Carmen's physical opposite—tall, thin, and blond. But that was a liability in a neighborhood where boobs and butt reigned supreme.

"I gave up on Eric a long time ago, I swear," Carmen insisted, but no one believed her. She had been obsessed with Iz's cousin, Eric, since he'd moved here from Brooklyn two years ago. He was undeniably hot, and had landed an impressive position as sous-chef at a fancy French restaurant. "He's a sous-chef I'd love to work under," Carmen always said, and we knew exactly what she meant.

Problem was, Eric had a serious girlfriend who'd moved all the way from Brooklyn to be with him. From what Iz had told us, they were solid.

"I told you, Carmen," Iz said, "you've got to do something about your guy karma. You keep obsessing over these really *good* guys. But good guys always have girlfriends, and they never cheat on them or dump them even if they're fifty shades of bitch."

Abby and I exchanged a knowing smile. Iz was speaking from experience—she was one of those bitches.

"I think you have great taste in guys, Carmen," I said.

"Yeah," Abby agreed. "It's a timing thing. You need to snag the guy *before* he gets a girl."

"Then she'll need to visit a junior high, for God's sake," Iz said. "The good ones get snatched up early."

She might be right. I hoped not.

Iz turned to Carmen. "Shake things up, mama! Get yourself a bad boy. He'll be so grateful to be with a girl like you without a dirty past, crying babies, and stretch marks. He'll straighten out his life, laser off his tats, and get himself a decent job. You'll see."

"I hear ya," Carmen said glumly, and took a long sip of margarita.

"Good, because all the guys coming tonight will be single except Rob." Iz looked at me. "I have someone in mind for you. Total hot tamale named Jack. I told Rob that if he's gonna come over, he *has* to bring him. Jack is in college, baby."

"Sounds promising," Abby said, gently nudging me. I sometimes envied her—she'd already found her forever guy, a nineteen-year-old marine named Kyle. They'd been together for three years. Five months ago he'd been deployed to Afghanistan, and he wrote to her almost every day.

Around midnight, Rob and four friends showed up, bringing in a gust of night air and cologne. Rob Velez was the star of the track team at Coral Gables High. He and Iz had met last fall when we'd crashed one of their school dances. The second he walked in the door, Rob pulled her close, whispering in her ear. It must have been something romantic, because Iz rolled her eyes and wriggled out of his arms, as if to say, "enough already." Poor Rob. He should know by now that Iz didn't have a romantic bone in her body.

"Let's introduce Maddie to Jack, okay?" Iz said, then grabbed the arm of a cute blond guy in a Heat jersey and marched him up to me like an early birthday present.

"Maddie, this is Jack. Jack, this is Maddie. Discuss."

I perked up. "Hey."

Jack looked me over and grinned. "Niiiice."

Ugh. In that one word, I knew who I was dealing with: an assclown frat boy. Did Iz actually think I'd go for a guy like him? Sometimes I wondered if she knew me at all.

With no clear escape route, I sat down with Jack and tried to have something resembling a conversation. I asked about college, and he launched into a disgusting story of dorm debauchery, worthy of a *Jackass* reunion movie. I glanced over at Carmen, who seemed to be having better luck. She'd cozied up to Rafael, a guy with a buzz cut and a serious way about him. Soon after, they were making out.

After wasting an hour of my life listening to Jack, I went to the bathroom, and took my time before returning. When I came back into the living room, I avoided his eyes and went over to sit with Abby in front of the TV. It seemed like the most painless way to show I wasn't interested.

By one thirty, Abby and I were dozing on top of each other. Which meant it was time to go.

As we stepped outside, Abby said, "That Jack guy was such a loser. Iz has no idea what type of guy you need. I'll set you up with one of Kyle's military friends when he gets back."

"Thanks." I didn't want to hurt her feelings, but I couldn't picture myself with a military boyfriend. I could never handle the worry and the loneliness. I'd be less lonely being single than missing a boyfriend overseas.

Abby and I headed off in different directions, and I cut through the park. It was especially quiet—even the late-night basketball players had called it quits. A homeless man sat on a bench muttering to himself. His name was Hector, and he'd been a fixture on these streets for as long as I could remember. He was often drunk, probably schizophrenic, and totally harmless.

I was startled when I spotted two guys on the play structure staring at me. Their gazes raised the little hairs on the back of my neck.

I took stock of them in the space of a second, noting their glazed eyes and tattoos, the beer bottles and crumpled food cartons at their feet. The one in the wifebeater had a cursive *R* on his bicep. It could only mean one thing in this neighborhood: Los Reyes. But from the look of them, I would've known that anyway.

I knew that I had to greet them in the right way—like I was flattered, but didn't want what they offered. If I looked away too quickly, if I showed my disgust, I'd offend them.

And you just didn't do that. Not to Reyes.

Maybe I should've listened to Mom and taken the bus. But I could walk home in the time it took to wait at the bus stop, so I hardly ever waited.

I walked by the play structure, feeling a quiver in my legs, bracing for them to shout something after me.

Seconds passed. I got farther away. Once I cleared the park, I breathed a sigh of relief.

There was far-off laughter, and I risked a glance over my shoulder. They'd turned their attention on Hector.

The Reyes grabbed Hector's bottle, hooting and hollering as they danced around him. He curled up, waving them away.

But they weren't going anywhere.

Without warning, the guy with the shaved head shoved him off the bench. They started kicking him.

Keep walking, I told myself. *You can't help him.*

My home was two blocks straight and another block right, but I slipped into an alley so I could keep an eye on Hector.

He was huddled in the fetal position. Kicks and punches rocked him side to side. He didn't resist, didn't even try to get away. For some reason, his passiveness only egged them on. It was like they were kicking around a rag doll.

My fingers trembled as I dialed 9-1-1.

"9-1-1. What's your emergency?"

"A man just got jumped in Emery Park. They've got him on the ground. They're kicking him."

"We're dispatching a unit right away, ma'am. Stay on the line with me, please."

"Okay." I felt so helpless, but I knew that if I got involved, the Reyes would turn on me.

And then they stopped. Hector was crumpled on the ground, not moving. He could be badly hurt. Where were the cops? They practically lived on every corner in this neighborhood. And now? Where were they?

"He's gonna need an ambulance," I told the dispatcher. "Hurry!"

One of the Reyes was dumping the contents of Hector's bottle all over him. I gritted my teeth. One last insult.

The guy with the shaved head took out a lighter. He stooped down next to Hector.

I froze. *Oh God, please don't. Please don't!*

"They're setting him on fire!" I shouted into the phone.

I ran toward Hector, screaming. The Reyes bolted from the scene.

I reached him in seconds. He bucked and twisted on the ground, the flames spreading all over him. I had no coat to smother them. I shouted, "Roll in the sand! The sand!"

He couldn't hear me. He was shrieking, whirling on the concrete. I tried to grab at his shirt so I could drag him to the sand. But wherever I gripped, the flames scalded me, and I kept letting go. I heard sirens, prayed for them to hurry up.

Seconds passed. Too many seconds.

Suddenly an EMT ran up and threw a blanket over him,

smothering the flames.

I stood there trembling as the EMTs worked on him.

They must've given him a shot of something, because by the time they'd loaded him up in the ambulance, he was quiet. So quiet.

People had come out of their homes and surrounded the scene. A cop materialized beside me, asking my name. I couldn't think. For several seconds I couldn't even answer him.

"M-Maddie. Diaz."

"You saw what happened?" the cop asked.

I nodded. "I—I should've stopped them."

It didn't even occur to me that people could see me talking to the cops.

WITNESS

I WAS IN A DARK ROOM, BREATHING in the scent of Hugo Boss. My arms were crossed over my chest, as if I could keep myself from falling apart.

"Take a good look at each one before you make your choice," Detective Gutierrez said. "There's no rush."

I didn't remember saying I would do this. After I'd talked to two cops at the crime scene, I thought I could go home. But they weren't done with me yet. They brought me in, let me quickly call my mom, and then they made me wait.

And wait.

And wait.

The lights came up behind the glass. Six men were lined up before a height wall. One of them was obviously drunk.

A couple looked pissed off. Another one was wild-eyed and high. And two of them, at opposite ends, had no expressions whatsoever. Their faces were stone cold.

One and six, I thought without hesitation. Number one had a shaved head, a soul patch on his chin, and an *R* tattoo on his arm. Number six had darker skin, hair in cornrows, and tattoos all over his arms and neck. But it wasn't only those details that made them easy to identify. It was the vibe they gave off, even now—a vibe that had put me on alert the second I saw them in the park.

"Are the men who set him on fire in this lineup?" Detective Gutierrez asked me.

They can't make you talk, said a voice in my head. *You don't have to do this.*

The cops had gotten a lot out of me while I was still in shock, before I'd had a chance to think. I'd let them carry me along, too overwhelmed to dig in my heels.

"I need a few minutes," I said.

"All right. I know you must be exhausted, Maddie. We'll take you right home after you make the IDs. Just tell me yes or no: are the perps here or not?"

And if I said no?

Lying was a mortal sin in my family. Lying is why Mom finally dumped Boyd after a thousand great reasons hadn't been enough. Sure, he drank away her money and put her down; sure, he'd hardly worked a day in his life. But when she caught him lying about going to his mother's place when he was really out gambling, that was it: the proof she needed.

The perp with the *R* tattoo, number one, was looking past the bright lights. For the second time tonight, he was staring right at me. Before, it was degrading and menacing. Now it was pure violence. I felt my hands shaking. Could he see me? I'd assumed it was one-way glass, but I wasn't so sure anymore.

"You're our only witness, as far as we know," Detective Gutierrez said. "The man who was burned, we know his name. It's Hector Rodriguez. He has family, you know. We've already spoken to his sister."

"I know who Hector is, okay?"

I couldn't believe I'd snapped at a cop. But I didn't care. I'd told him I needed to think, and he kept putting on the pressure.

"I'll be back in a few minutes," he finally said.

Then it was me, alone in the darkness, with number one and number six. It felt like they could crash through the glass at any moment and strangle me. Suddenly I wished I hadn't let the detective go.

As if he'd heard my thoughts, Detective Gutierrez returned. "Just got word from the hospital. Hector Rodriguez is dead."

The floor seemed to wobble beneath me, and I had to

steady myself with a chair. *Oh my God. Poor Hector.* Tears came to my eyes. Those psycho motherfuckers.

I took a breath and turned to him. "It's one and six. And yeah, I'm sure."

Gutierrez nodded grimly. "Thank you."

Maybe he understood what I'd just done. I wasn't sure if I did.

AFTERMATH

"HI, TOM. I WON'T BE COMING IN TODAY." I didn't have to try to make my voice weak and grumbly—it came out that way.

"Heard what happened," Tom shouted over the noise and beeping in the background. "I said two orders of *large* fries, not small!"

I closed my eyes. Even my half-senile boss had heard about last night. That meant *everyone* in the neighborhood knew. Everyone.

"So is it okay if I stay home today?"

There was a pause. Then, "Hey, back on cash now! Sure, Maddie, that's fine. We'll see you tomorrow."

It was two o'clock in the afternoon, and I'd just woken up. I didn't want to get out of bed. I didn't want to be conscious.

Mom came in. She must've called in sick too because she usually worked Saturdays at the hotel. "Heard you on the phone. Did you get some sleep?"

"Yeah."

Mom sat on the side of my bed and cradled me against her. She'd been awake when I got home last night, waiting for me.

"What you need is some good food. I made huevos rancheros."

"Thanks, Mom." The last thing I felt like was a big, heavy breakfast meant for farmworkers. But I knew she must have spent a while making it, so I'd better have some.

I took a shower, then joined her in the kitchen. My plate was piled high. Mom showed love through food. She could never afford to spoil me with clothes, high tech gadgets, or music lessons, so food was her only option. She had spoiled Dad, too, and he'd loved her cooking too much to say no. Which was probably why he'd ended up with type 2 diabetes. After his death, I'd learned to say no to the food. Good thing I had, too. Once I'd hit puberty and started to get serious curves, I'd had to watch what I ate.

I took a few bites before Mom said, "Iz keeps calling to check on you."

"I'll call her." It had been a rough night for everyone. When I hadn't texted Iz to say I'd gotten home safe, she'd called Mom. They'd been about to go look for me when I called Mom from the police station. I'd desperately wanted to contact the girls, too, but I'd dropped my phone at the scene, and the cops wouldn't let me call anyone but Mom. I knew why. They didn't want me in contact with anyone who might encourage me *not* to talk.

I wouldn't be surprised if the cops had found my phone and chosen not to give it back to me. It didn't matter now. I wasn't going back to the park to look for it.

The park.

A thousand jumbled images flashed before my eyes. Detective Gutierrez's words echoed in my head. *Hector Rodriguez is dead.*

I should've intervened when they were beating him up. I should've screamed and brought down the attention of the whole neighborhood. Should've, should've, should've . . .

But I was a coward.

"Maddie?" my mom said gently.

I realized I was gripping the edge of the table. "Sorry, Mom. I don't feel like eating."

That's when I broke down.

Iz was a great distracter, I had to give her that. When I texted her saying I wasn't up to seeing anyone that night, she didn't text back. Instead, she showed up at my door with Abby and Carmen and a juice container full of leftover Maddie Diaz Margaritas. She told my mom it was Crystal Light.

I was so touched, I wanted to cry. Iz knew that I hated to be alone. During the Boyd years, she'd been my saving grace. Her house had been my refuge.

Me and the girls went to the basement to watch TV and to escape my mom. She'd been hovering all day, wanting to talk. But I didn't. How could I when I hadn't even processed what had happened? When it still didn't feel real?

The second we sat down, Carmen said, "You don't have to tell us about last night if you don't want to. But if you do, we're here for you."

Abby stared at her. "We agreed not to mention it. And it's the first thing you do!"

"I know, but she might *want* to talk about it," Carmen snapped back. "We're not helping her if we ignore it."

"She'll bring it up if she wants to, okay?" Iz said.

I raised my hand. "Guys, I'm right here. I'm not allowed to talk about what I saw. All I can say is that I identified the guys who did it, and they're gonna be charged. That's it."

My friends gasped.

"You ID'd them?" Abby asked slowly, like she couldn't believe what I was saying. "Aren't you worried that ..."

"That they'll come after me? Yeah, I'm worried." Worried

didn't begin to describe how I felt. Worried. Guilty. *Sick.*

"Don't be," Iz said, squeezing my hand. "Everybody knows you talked to the cops and that's your best protection. If any of the Reyes touch you, the cops would know it was them. They're not that stupid."

I wasn't sure if she meant it or if she was just trying to make me feel better. But I *had* to believe what she was saying. If I didn't, I'd never leave the house again.

I put up the volume on the TV, and we all turned our attention to some music videos. Or pretended to. Finally Abby broke the silence.

"So, Carmen. What happened with Rafael after we left?"

Carmen's lips curled into a smile. "I decided to take Iz's advice and shake up my guy karma. He's supposed to call me next week."

I hoped Rafael called her. Carmen had been disappointed by too many guys, and it was about time her luck changed.

"Jack told me you blew him off," Iz said to me. "You didn't like him?"

"He was obnoxious. What does he study in college, anyway? Dick Jokes 101?"

"I think it's *Douche*-ology," Abby said, and we bumped fists.

"Whatevs." Iz pointed her finger at me. "I'm not done with you, Maddie."

After chatting and watching a few more videos, Carmen

suggested we hit the store for some eats. My pulse shot up at the thought of leaving the house. I suddenly pictured the two Reyes waiting for me in an alley, ready to go at me with baseball bats.

I shoved the thought aside. Those guys were locked up and wouldn't be getting out on bail anytime soon—Detective Gutierrez had assured me of that. I couldn't shut myself away from the world because of last night.

Still, I brought Dex with us. I had no doubt he'd rip to shreds anyone who tried something with me. Thanks to Boyd, Dex hated all men. When I took him on walks, he growled at every guy who passed by. That was why my friends never let me take him to the store with us, since cruising for guys was part of the point.

But tonight, they didn't protest.

Sasso's Variety was three blocks away. It was open twenty-four hours, three hundred and sixty-five days a year, and had been robbed more times than I could count. It had cameras everywhere now and was probably more secure than the local Citibank. There was a No Dogs Allowed sign on the door, so I tied Dex up outside.

Dex bared his teeth to a group of b-ballers with sports drinks, and they moved a few feet away. Beyond them, a homeless woman sat cross-legged with a cardboard box of change in front of her. I'd seen Hector here so many times.

An image of his flaming body rose up in my mind. I shook my head, trying to dislodge it.

We went inside, the shop's doorbell dinging above us. I glanced behind the counter. Unfortunately, the good-looking cashier was working. He always seemed to be working when I was buying something embarrassing, like tampons or junk food, or when I looked sloppy, like when I was buying milk early in the morning. That was *my* guy karma.

My friends buzzed at the sight of him—unruly black hair, a chiseled, clean-shaven face. He wore a faded T-shirt and jeans, and had tanned, muscular arms unmarred by tattoos. Nobody knew his name, since this wasn't the sort of store where you wore a name tag, but it didn't matter—they appreciated him as pure, unadulterated guy candy.

We went to the chip/candy aisle and filled a basket with whatever looked appealing. I heard Dex barking. My heart leaped into my throat, and I darted a look outside. But Dex was just being Dex, doing his best to intimidate a grizzled guy having a smoke.

Damn it. Was I always going to be this jumpy?

As we moved around the store, I sensed eyes following us. It was the guy at the register. Did he think we were shoplifting? We'd been here enough for him to know that wasn't our M.O.

When I glanced up, his gaze moved away. Of course. It

was *me* he was watching. He must know I was the girl. The witness.

We went up to the counter and unloaded the basket. Iz adjusted her red bra strap, which was sticking to her skin—one of her classic moves. "Muggy out, huh?"

"Yeah," he said.

Okay, I had to admit, I liked that he had always seemed immune to Iz. She knew it, too, and that only made her try harder.

"Working the graveyard tonight?" she asked.

He looked at her like he wanted to say, "Duh," but instead he said, "Yeah."

Abby turned to me, desperate not to laugh at Iz's failure. I sputtered, and when the guy glanced at me, I turned it into a cough. His hazel eyes met mine for a long beat before looking away.

"Must be a long, hard night for you," Carmen said.

My mouth dropped open. We expected this from Iz, but never from Carmen. Last night with Rafael must have boosted her confidence.

"It takes stamina." His lips twitched, like he was trying not to smile. "But it's no problem for me. I can go all night."

Abby's nails dug into my arm as we both fought laughter. Carmen threw a glance at Iz, victorious. She'd gotten him to play along, and it was only her first try.

Outside, Dex bounded high when he saw us. I untied him, glancing back through the glass. The guy behind the counter was still watching me.

Guess I'd have to get used to it.

LOCA

MOM SAID I SHOULD HAVE COUNSELING. That I was suffering from PTSD. That my "faith in humanity had been shattered by witnessing such a horrible crime." It was a pretty impressive diagnosis, and a testament to her faithful watching of Dr. Drew.

She was probably right.

I had seen a shrink a few times after Dad's death—or a *grief counselor,* as she'd called herself, but it was all the same to me. She'd kept asking me about that day, about how it felt to be brought home from school early by my grandmother, only to be told that my dad had died of a heart attack. The shrink wanted to know how I, as an eleven-year-old, was handling this trauma. But all I'd wanted was to stop being pressured to put words to a grief I had no words for.

Now Mom was insisting that I see someone again. So the following week I made an appointment with the school psychologist. It would at least confirm to everyone at school that I was in desperate need of psychological help. Why else would I, Maddie Diaz, a supposedly smart girl and editor of the school newspaper, *Prep Talk*, have ratted on two Reyes?

Because I was batshit crazy, of course.

I was just lucky that I didn't go to my neighborhood school. If I were at Rivera with Carmen and Abby, I'd be a target. Rivera was full of gangbangers, some of them affiliated with the Reyes.

Thursday at lunch was the school newspaper meeting. I was tempted to reschedule it for next week, but I couldn't bring myself to do it. I had enough trouble chasing everyone down for their articles as it was, and any delay would only make it worse.

Although I'd been on the newspaper staff since I was a freshman, I'd never dreamed of being editor. I had enough on my plate with trying to maintain my GPA and working on weekends. But last September Ms. Halsall, the staff advisor to the newspaper, had suggested I go for it. She'd said that being editor would look great on a college application, and that my writing was "incisive and brave." I hadn't even known what *incisive* meant, but I knew why she'd called it brave. I'd written an article on girl trafficking in Miami, and people *still* talked about it.

Since everybody on staff knew that I could write, I got elected. The thing was, no one knew if I could lead. Including me.

At first, running the meetings had scared the hell out of me. Although my voice was steady, I could feel my knees trembling. But I made it through those first few weeks, and proved to myself that I really was cut out for this. Once I'd figured that out, my knees stopped shaking.

When the noon bell rang, everybody flooded in. For once, all ten of them showed up.

"Hey, guys, let's get started." I looked around. "Who's doing the film and TV section for the April edition?"

Brad raised his hand. "I'll do it."

"Everybody cool with that?" I asked. "Great. Now, I think we should do Part Five of *Staff Stories*. You can choose whoever you want, but I bet Ms. Karpoff would be interesting. She grew up in Romania, post World War Two."

"I'll do it, but I want to write about Mr. Marshall," Samantha said. "He's got all these stories from the Gulf War."

"Awesome. Now, for the social issues section."

When I paused to take a breath, Cassidy jumped in. "You have to do social issues this time, Maddie. Everybody wants to know exactly what happened with that homeless guy. And it could be a jumping-off point for a discussion of gang violence. Didn't you say in the fall we should write about that?"

Leave it to Cassidy to bring up the one thing I wasn't ready to talk about—or write about.

The room was so quiet you could hear a pin drop. Maybe *this* was why attendance was so good today. Everyone wanted the story.

"I can't write about it for legal reasons," I said.

"Does that mean you're gonna testify?" asked Josh, the sports writer.

I nodded.

"Maybe they'll cover the trial on TV," said a freshman named Arleth. "You could be famous!"

"It's not going to be on TV," I said. I hadn't even considered that. "Anyway, let's move on to the—"

"Even if you can't get specific about the case, you should still write an article about gangs," Cassidy said. "Don't you want to bring attention to the problem?"

My face heated up. In true Cassidy style, she wouldn't take no for an answer. She'd given me a hard time ever since I became editor, a position she'd desperately wanted. Her greatest wish was to make me look incompetent.

Right now, she'd settled for making me look insensitive. I glanced at Ms. Halsall, who sat up on a desk, eating carrot sticks. Forty-something and hip, she had a streak of gray at the front of her wild red hair. Ms. Halsall watched me intently, not sparing a glance at Cassidy. It reminded me that I was the one in charge here.

I wasn't going to let Cassidy force me into an *I'm not in the right space to write about this* speech. I was the editor, right?

"I've already started work on a two-parter about transitioning to college," I said, turning away from Cassidy. "Anyone want to do an article on gang violence, as she suggested?"

There were no takers.

"Cassidy, what about you?" I asked.

"I can't, I'm covering the spring play."

"All right, then. Moving along."

I caught a glimmer of approval in Ms. Halsall's eyes. For once, I'd managed to shut Cassidy down.

That night, the doorbell rang. Dex went wild, launching himself at the front door, scratching and barking. I peered through the peephole.

Detective Gutierrez. I was surprised that he was showing up at seven o'clock at night, but then, this was probably the start of his shift. He was driving an unmarked car, not that it mattered much. The whole neighborhood already knew I'd been talking to the cops.

Although Gutierrez was a solid, stocky guy, the sound of

Dex's barking made him scoot back from the door.

"Just a second!" I put Dex out back, then returned to open the door. "Sorry, he gets excited."

"A dog like that's better than any burglar alarm," he said, walking in. He wore crisp office clothes and looked freshly shaved. "We use German shepherds in our canine units. They're smart dogs."

"I know." I led him to the living room, which was messy with dog toys and Mom's tabloids. My laptop and the remains of my dinner sat on the coffee table.

"I'm sorry to bother you, Maddie. But I wanted to update you on what's happening."

I moved a copy of *Us Weekly* off the couch and we both sat down.

"The two men you identified, Ramon Santiago and Diego Gomez, were arraigned earlier this week and charged with second-degree murder."

"I know. Saw it on the news."

"Judge Conway set their bonds at a million dollars. We're looking at a trial date of August seventeenth of next year."

"Next year?" I wanted this over yesterday, not next year.

"The timeline's standard, unfortunately. You'll need to be available for at least a week, maybe more. The DA's office will be in touch with you long before that to go over your testimony and coach you on what to expect on the witness stand."

"All right." I'd seen enough crime shows to know how it works.

He cleared his throat. "You'll be an excellent witness, Maddie. You've got the confidence not to let the defense cut you down." He gave a meaningful pause. "You did the right thing by speaking out."

Of course I had. But hearing him say it didn't bring me any comfort. It felt like there was an unsaid ending to his statement: *You did the right thing despite what the Reyes might do to you.*

"Am I in danger?" I asked, flat out.

He took his time in answering. "If some of the gang members come after you, it will only make things worse for Ramon and Diego. But you never know about these guys. My advice is to stay in public places. No more walking through the park after midnight."

Darn, no more moonlight strolls. But in all fairness, what could he say? *No worries, you're safe?* Or *Good luck, it's just a matter of time?*

"Now, I have to get going, unless you have any questions for me."

I hesitated. There was something else I needed to know. "Was there a funeral for Hector? I didn't hear about one on the news." The moment I spoke his name, my throat seized up. I tried not to think about him, about his suffering, about his family. But it was always there, lingering beneath the surface.

"I believe his family held a service," he said, then stood up.

"Good." Hector deserved that, at least.

Before he stepped outside, Gutierrez said, "Don't forget, Maddie, you can't share details of the case with anyone. If anything is leaked, your credibility will come into question. And our whole case is resting on your testimony."

"Don't worry, Detective. I get it."

FRIDAY NIGHT

THE NEXT NIGHT, I SAT BY MYSELF, slowly working through my medium fries.

The staff room looked like a cramped locker room, its walls splattered with forty years of McDonald's propaganda. There was even a life-size Ronald McDonald statue, his hands cupped like he was praying. Creepy. I could never sit facing the thing, for fear old Ronald would wink at me.

The door swung open. "Diaz! I was missing you."

"Hey." I hadn't seen Manny since last Friday, and I'd actually missed joking around with him.

He slipped his uniform on over his T-shirt, then plunked down beside me. "I been worried about you."

For once, Manny wasn't joking.

"I'm okay. It was a horrible thing, you know?"

"I know." And I could tell that he did. You didn't get tattoos like that without having witnessed a few things yourself.

"Everybody thinks I have a death wish because I talked to the police. It wasn't like that. I had to talk about what I saw." I looked at him. He knew about gangs, didn't he? Maybe I should ask. "Do you think the Reyes will come after me? I heard their leader is . . . brutal." Which was the mildest way I could say it.

Manny didn't miss a beat. "Salazar doesn't give a shit about you, Maddie. He's not gonna lose sleep over Ramon and Diego. He's got a lot of guys like them. They were small-time, trust me."

Just the name Salazar made my stomach sick. He was the head of the Reyes, a kingpin who dealt in drugs, guns, and girls. His name had come up many times when I'd researched girl trafficking for my article last year. Not that I had dared name him in print.

"Salazar's got his hands full these days," Manny said. "He's got a cartel from Tijuana trying to put him out of business. Plus, his dealers are getting robbed left and right. No one even knows who's behind it. Some say it's an underground gang. Point is, you're not even a small fish to him. You're, like, a fucking guppy."

I smiled. I'd never been so happy to be called a fucking

guppy. I only wished I'd talked to Manny days ago. I might have slept better if I had.

"Do you know them, Ramon and Diego?"

He shrugged one shoulder. "Yeah, kinda. We're from the same neighborhood. Never liked them, though."

"So you don't think they're . . . planning something. I mean, without Salazar."

"If Ramon and Diego wanted to get you, they probably would've done it by now. They could've easily called up their friends and told them to burn your house down. No planning necessary."

That wasn't so comforting. It had only been a week. Maybe Ramon and Diego were slackers when it came to exacting revenge.

"Be careful, though. Reyes are all over the place. You see one coming, you step out of their way. Don't go starting something."

"I won't, trust me."

"What you need"—he bent closer, and I could smell his spicy aftershave—"is a personal driver." He put a hand to his chest. "I'll be your guy."

"I'll take you up on that sometime. Not tonight, though. My friends are picking me up in a cab. We're going to Iz's cousin's party."

"Next time, then. I'll take you anywhere you wanna go,

Diaz." He winked. "Anywhere."

I had to smile. He wouldn't be Manny if he didn't try.

Now this is a party.

It was exactly what I'd pictured college parties would be like—low lighting, acid jazz on the Bose. A stylish crowd was hanging out, some of them dancing, some lounging, some cradling glasses of sangria between their legs.

"Hey, you guys showed up." Eric came out of the kitchen, wiping his hands on a dish towel. The aromas of cumin, garlic, and other spices wafted toward us.

"That smells incredible," Iz said, giving her cousin a hug and glancing past him into the kitchen. "Is it ready?"

"Almost." With Eric's good looks and Brooklyn accent, I couldn't blame Carmen for crushing on him. I'd have crushed, too, if there'd been any point. "Here comes my girl, Julia." Eric's girlfriend walked out of the kitchen. She had wavy dark hair, big earrings and a warm smile. I liked her immediately. He slung an arm around her, and looked down at her proudly. "She goes to U. of M. for creative writing."

We all said hi. I glanced at Carmen. If she was upset to meet Julia, she didn't show it. I guess she was finally past her Eric fantasy, probably because she'd gone out with Rafael twice this week.

Within minutes, we were all drinking Eric's homemade sangria. Heavy on fruit and light on alcohol, I bet this was his way of keeping the party under control. Me and the girls went into the living room, and since we didn't know anyone, we danced. I loved the music and danced hard, wanting nothing more than to lose myself in it. And I was pretty much succeeding until I saw him.

Him. Corner Store Guy. He was sitting across the room with a group of guys, watching me. I glanced over my shoulder to make sure he wasn't looking at some hot chick behind me. When I looked back, he was staring down at his phone.

I had to admit, the sight of him made my heartbeat kick up. It was either that or the dancing/sangria combo. I promised myself that I'd talk to him at some point. I couldn't strike out worse than Iz had last weekend.

The dancing continued, and after a bathroom break, I lost track of the girls. They were probably in the kitchen feasting on Eric's arroz con pollo. Instead of searching for them, I wandered into one of the bedrooms and found myself listening in on some philosophical chat. It was an interesting mix of people—one of Eric's roommates and his girlfriend, along with a few people who worked at Eric's restaurant.

College could be like this, I thought. Great parties and conversation. I just had to make it till September, and then I was outta here.

"Heard you're a writer too." A girl sat down beside me. It was Julia.

"Well, not a creative writer like you. Respect to that. I'm studying journalism next year."

"I know. Iz was bragging about your scholarship to Florida State. Ever since I met her she's been bragging about you."

"That's Iz. She probably made most of it up." I searched for something to say. "Miami must be really different from Brooklyn, huh?"

"Hell, yeah. But I love it here. The palm trees, the beach. It's a total paradise compared to Brooklyn."

"I'd love to go there sometime. I've heard it's the most amazing place."

"It is, but . . ." She sighed. "I was ready to leave. Junior year of high school was kind of crazy. My dad and I ended up moving to Queens so I could finish. It just wasn't the same. Brooklyn will always be where I'm from, but it's not home anymore."

I wanted to ask what crazy stuff she was referring to, but I doubted she wanted to spill it. Whatever it was, it sounded like trouble. And Julia didn't seem the type to get into trouble.

"I feel the same, in a way," I said. "My mom married this asshole and it's been a rough ride ever since. She finally woke up, but he's stalling the divorce. I've been dying to leave Miami. To start over." I was surprised at myself for being so open, but why not? I liked her. "Moving to Tallahassee's just what I need."

She nodded, like she totally got me.

A game of poker started, and we headed back to the living room. There was a huge piece of artwork on the wall, a gritty Miami street scene. Julia told me how Eric had brought the canvas to his favorite street artist and paid him fifty bucks to do it. I guess having an eye for art was something Eric and Iz had in common.

Julia sat down on one of the couches, and shooed away a guy so that I could sit.

"These are Eric's boxing buddies," she explained.

One of them was Corner Store Guy. He was sitting on a chair next to the couch, beer in hand. When our eyes met, he actually said, "Hey."

Julia noticed. "You know Ortiz?"

Ortiz. So that was his name.

"I—we've—at the store." Way to impress a guy. I hoped the darkness masked my red cheeks.

"He and Eric beat the shit out of each other last week," Julia said, glaring at him. "I wasn't impressed."

"That's 'cause you didn't see it," Ortiz said, a glint in his hazel eyes. "You missed a fight, Julia."

"I didn't miss the bruises. Why can't you guys play tennis, or something that doesn't leave you messed up?"

"Tennis wouldn't feed the beast. Your man Eric's got the Brooklyn in him."

"I've got it in *me*, too," Julia threw back at him. "Next time no black eyes, 'kay? I don't think his boss at the restaurant was too happy about it."

"Deal." That's when Ortiz turned my way. To my surprise, he reached out his hand. "Maddie Diaz, right?"

"Yeah." His palm was callused, a boxer's hand. I felt a shiver go up my arm.

"You have some funny friends," he said, his mouth curving up. "You're not like them, are you?"

I smiled. I suspected he was flirting with me, but I couldn't be sure.

"I heard all about you, Maddie Diaz. I admire what you did."

I was startled that he brought it up. I couldn't accept the compliment, though. "Don't admire me. I didn't do enough. I wish . . ." I broke off. The intense look in his eyes silenced me.

"You told the truth," he said.

I couldn't argue with that. And I had to admit, Ortiz's praise meant a lot. No one else had reacted that way to what I'd done. They'd reacted with worry, horror, or curiosity. Never admiration. Not even my mom.

"Hector practically lived outside the store," he said. "I used to give him overstock before we threw it out, and he was always grateful. The guy was more polite than most customers."

A lump rose in my throat. "I can believe it."

I felt a hand on my shoulder—Julia's.

"Maddie's a writer, you know," Julia said, abruptly changing the topic. "She did this whole exposé on girl trafficking in Miami."

I glanced at Julia, part *thank you*, part *you didn't have to do that*. I guess Iz really had been bragging about me.

Ortiz nodded gravely. "I heard about the problem. Girls lured from everywhere with promises of a better life. So, Maddie Diaz. Did you find a solution?"

"I wish. Mainly it's putting the information out there to warn the girls before they get sucked in."

"What about getting them out?"

"That's the problem. They're so hard to find. By the time the cops get enough tips to search a place, they've been moved somewhere else."

Since Ortiz looked interested in what I was saying, I kept going. I glanced at Julia, but she'd slipped away. It was girl code at its best: get the conversation going, then leave us to talk. She must've sensed that something could happen between us. Or was it just me?

Ortiz asked more questions. He had this sexy way of scrunching up his eyes when he was thinking, but it wasn't put on. He was a very smart guy. I couldn't help but wonder if he was in college, or if he planned on going. I was about to ask him when he pulled out his phone—a conversation killer if there ever was one.

"Sorry," he said, cutting me off. "Gotta go."

"Oh, okay." Suddenly I felt vulnerable. But I mustered up a smile, hoping he'd ask for my number.

Ortiz got up. He said, "Later" to his friends, then he left.

I stared after him, sinking into the couch. All I could think was, *Are you kidding me?*

We hit up an all-night Denny's for the party postmortem. Except for Carmen—she hailed a cab to drop her off at Rafael's place.

"Ba-ba-booty call!"

Iz was the one who shouted it. But I was thinking it. I bet Abby was, too.

Carmen grinned and waved us off as she got into the cab. She'd go back to Iz's later. Since Carmen's parents were strict with curfews, she slept over there a lot. As for my mom, she was easy as long as she knew where I was and who I was with. I texted her to say I'd be home within an hour and that I'd share a cab with the girls.

Denny's was full of Friday night partyers. The lights were

too bright, and neither Iz's nor Abby's makeup had survived intact. I doubted mine had either.

"I'm talking chicken wings, cheese sticks, and calamari," Iz declared. "Two appetizer platters?"

We were all over that. It went without saying that we'd order the greasiest food possible. It was necessary to soak up the alcohol.

"I'm not feeling this Rafael," Abby said, licking honey garlic sauce off her fingers. "I don't know why Carmen's so into him. It's too early in their relationship for a booty call."

"Relationship and booty call don't belong in the same sentence," I said. "I hope she's not expecting more." I wasn't at all sure Carmen was playing this right. But since she was hypersensitive, I knew better than to question her.

"Rafael is exactly what she needs," Iz said. "She's always falling for guys who don't look twice at her. It's about time she's reminded that she's a quality girl." A grin took over her lips. "I bet he's reminding her right now." She savored her chicken wing a little too enthusiastically, and we all laughed.

Abby looked at me. "So tell me what happened with cute cashier guy."

"His name's Ortiz. Julia introduced us. Turns out he boxes with Eric."

"I love a guy who goes by his last name," Iz said. "That is so classic."

"And?" Abby said. "Did you give him your number?"

"He didn't ask. Actually, he left really fast. He looked at his phone and then he was gone."

Iz nearly choked on her chicken wing. "No way. That is so rude!"

"It doesn't mean he wasn't into you," Abby said. "It could've been an emergency."

Iz scoffed. "Or it could've been his girlfriend."

"Maybe he just wanted to avoid the *I'll call you* thing," I said. "I don't know. But I'm not buying anything from Sasso's for at least two weeks."

"I've always thought he was full of himself," Iz said. "Next time I go there, I'm pouring a Slush Puppie over his head."

SHADOW

THAT NIGHT I DREAMED OF ORTIZ. I dreamed that I was watching him box, mesmerized by his ripped body and the sheer power of his punches. And then we drove off and found a cozy motel room.

That's when I woke up—before things got really good.

I lay back in bed. Couldn't I fantasize about someone who *hadn't* rejected me in the last twenty-four hours?

I took a shower, my vanilla body wash stripping off the remains of last night. I stood in the stream of hot water, trying not to relive scenes from the dream. Trying to forget what it felt like to be wanted, no, *needed*, like that.

Although I hadn't admitted it to the girls, I'd actually thought Ortiz was into me. Not burning for me, exactly, but interested. Who was I kidding? It was our topic of conversation he was interested in, not the rest of the package.

Which is probably why I was the editor of *Prep Talk* instead of the homecoming queen.

Cornflakes. After last night's drinking and greasy eats, they were all I could handle. I turned on the E! channel to enjoy the latest celebrity hot mess, and sat down on the couch, trying to get comfortable. All of our furniture was old and too soft, especially the couch, which was lopsided—thanks to two hundred and fifty pounds of Boyd practically living on it for three years.

Dex curled up beside me. Since Mom was at work, we had the place to ourselves for a while. It was nice.

Mom was smothering me these days, and I didn't like it. Weird. When Boyd had been in our lives, all I'd wanted was more of Mom's attention. Now that I had it, I didn't want it.

My phone rang. I had input all of my friends into my new phone, but I didn't recognize this number.

I caught my breath. "Hello?"

"Hey, Maddie. It's Julia."

I was an idiot. Of course it wasn't Ortiz. But this was also a surprise. "Hey."

"Hope I'm not calling too early."

"Not at all, I was awake." I perked myself up. I wanted Julia to know that I was glad she was calling me. "How late did the party go last night?"

"I'm not sure. Eric and I crashed around three, but some people stayed longer. We're done cleaning up and are going to Cosmo's for breakfast. Or brunch, I guess. Wanna come?"

Julia and Eric wanted to hang with me? Wow. "I'd love to, but I can't. I have to work at one."

"No probs. Oh, and I wanted to see how things went with Ortiz. He's cool, don't you think?"

This was embarrassing. "Yeah, he is. But he got a text and took off really fast."

"I kinda noticed that. Don't take it personally. Eric says Ortiz is always bolting. Maybe he's got ADHD."

"It's not a big deal."

"Anyway, Eric's about to chew his arm off here so I gotta go. But let's do it another time, okay? I'll call you."

"Sounds awesome."

I had to smile. Last night hadn't been a total loss after all.

Someone was watching me. I could feel it.

I glanced over my shoulder, but saw nothing. From the moment I'd walked out of McDonald's, I'd felt vulnerable.

It was 9:06 p.m. The bus was due in four minutes. I stood, waiting, in the midst of a group of harmless-looking people.

Abruptly I turned my head and saw a shadow hovering in

the alley. Then it was gone. Had I imagined it?

So much for Manny's offer to be my personal driver. He'd called in sick tonight. I needed him right now. I needed someone. Actually, the one I needed was Dex. I felt safe with him by my side, like nothing could touch me.

Three girls in their twenties were standing nearby, dressed for a night out—tight clothes, slicked-back hair, huge earrings, and oceans of perfume.

"You heard about Juan getting jumped last week?" one girl said.

"Jumped? They rolled his ass bad. Took all his cash and supply. Musta had him staked out." She cracked her gum. "It had to be the Destinos."

The short one disagreed. "You believe that shit? There's no such thing as the Destinos. It's an urban myth. My mom said there was a gang just like them in the eighties."

The girl scoffed. "The Reyes weren't even around in the eighties. And they're *only* fucking with Reyes. How do you explain that?"

Her friend was stumped.

The Destinos gang was the talk of the neighborhood. I didn't care if they were a real gang or a couple of rogue thugs, I was just glad that they were brave enough (or stupid enough) to give the Reyes a hard time. Hopefully they were higher on the Reyes hit list than I was.

I'm a fucking guppy, I reminded myself. It was my mantra, thanks to Manny.

I spotted movement from the corner of my eye, and my heart rate spiked. A young guy was walking toward the bus stop—toward *me*. He was a bit older than me and dressed clean-cut, but who knew what his story was?

The guy's eyes met mine. I was ready to run the second he made a move toward me.

I stood there, full of adrenaline. He looked me up and down, kind of smiled, and walked by. My heart was beating out of my chest.

My worst fears were confirmed. I was going crazy.

"I think I'm being followed," I told the school psychologist on Monday morning.

There, I'd said it. I would never tell my mom, because she'd freak out. I couldn't tell my friends, because they'd say I was being paranoid. And I couldn't go to Detective Gutierrez, because I had no proof.

But I could say it to Jennifer. She'd made it clear that I could say anything. No judgment.

This was only my second visit with her, but I'd decided that she was trustworthy. Which didn't mean I felt a connection with her. She was too clinical. She only had a handful of facial expressions, from the sensitive nod to the almost-smile to the compassionate brow furrow.

"Followed?" Her blue eyes opened a fraction wider, then she gave the sensitive nod. "Tell me more about that."

"Ever since the incident I've felt like I was being watched. When I'm at the bus stop. Or walking somewhere with Dex."

"Do you feel this way when you're in a safe place, say at home or"—she subtly glanced down at her notes—"at your friend Iz's house?"

I thought about it. "Not really. I mean, sometimes I worry that my house'll be set on fire, but that's just because a friend suggested it. I don't think anyone's looking through my window or anything. It's mostly when I'm outside."

"Have you spoken to Detective Gutierrez about this?"

I shook my head. "I don't see what he can do."

"But don't you think he'd want to know?"

"Maybe but . . ." This was the strange part, the embarrassing part. "Whoever they are, I don't think they're out to get me."

She raised an eyebrow. "That surprises me, in light of what you've been through."

"I know it's weird." Weird didn't begin to cover it. "Did you ever see that Oprah rerun with the 'gift of fear' stuff? My mom made me watch it. It's all about how your instincts know when there's a predator. Even if it's not rational, that feeling is there. But I don't feel any of that. Not like . . ."

She leaned forward in her chair. "Not like what?"

"The Reyes at the park. I knew right away that they were dangerous. That I had to get away from them."

She glanced down at her notes. "I want to go back to something you said. You said, *they're* not out to get you. Plural."

She was sharp, all right. "Sometimes I think it's more than one person. I mean, *different* people. Do I sound crazy?"

"Absolutely not," she said emphatically. "The sense of being followed is very common when you're experiencing post-traumatic stress."

Okay, so I wasn't crazy, I was just stressed. Post-traumatically stressed.

"So you don't think . . . it could be real?"

She gazed back at me, her blue eyes intense. "What do *you* think?"

That was the problem. I didn't trust my own judgment anymore. And I could tell she didn't either.

THE RING

IT DIDN'T GET ANY BETTER THAN THIS. I sat on a bench, the salty beach air blowing on my face. It was seven o'clock at night, still light out, and I was eating a taco.

"Holy shit, this is good," Julia said. "When you said you wanted tacos from a truck, I was doubting." As she took another bite, half of her taco fell into the tray. I held back a smile. If she was going to survive in Miami, she'd better learn how to eat a taco.

"Food trucks are big here," I said.

"Not in Flatbush, where I come from. If you're buying street eats, you'd better be packing Pepto Bismol."

I laughed, glad I wasn't holed up at home tonight. I'd been expecting a boring night of school newspaper editing when

Julia had called. No way I was going to pass up another invite. Besides, even if I'd have to stay up late working, tomorrow was Friday.

As we ate, I scanned my surroundings. Nothing unusual. Women in bikini tops and their bare-chested boyfriends rollerbladed by us. Tourists strolled, vendors hawked overpriced T-shirts. If the Reyes were planning to strike at me, they wouldn't do it here on the bustling boardwalk with so many witnesses.

At least, I hoped not.

At the end of my last visit, the school psychologist had suggested I take some anti-anxiety meds. Weird, because I thought psychologists weren't into that pharma shit.

No, thank you, I'd told her. I might be a little crazy these days, but the real crazy thing would be to dull my God-given senses.

"See someone you know?" Julia asked, picking up some taco entrails and popping them into her mouth.

Guess I wasn't so subtle after all. "Um, no. Just people watching."

"I know what it's like, Maddie. Back in Brooklyn, I got on the wrong side of the Bloods."

I gaped at her. "How'd that happen?"

"I heard Eric was going to get jumped, and I warned him. In the ghetto, that's snitching. I'm sure you can relate."

"Oh my God. The Bloods came after you?"

She nodded. "So I joined the Crips."

"What?" I couldn't picture smart, classy Julia as a gang member. No way.

"It's true," she said. "Anyway, that's ancient history. Point is, I know how it feels to be on your guard all the time. After I got jumped the first time, I was never really the same."

The first time? I didn't even know what to say.

"My theory is that a little paranoia's good for you. Keeps you alert." She closed up the remains of her taco and tossed it in the trash. "I have an idea. Let's go somewhere where you won't have to look over your shoulder."

"Sure. You lead the way."

We got on a crowded bus heading downtown. Julia told me about U. of M., about how much she loved her classes. But she said it wasn't always easy to meet people—the downside of living in an apartment off campus. The upside was that it was cheaper, she could cook her own food, and she and Eric could have as many sleepovers as they wanted.

It was so cool that Julia wanted to get to know me. I felt sort of bad that she didn't have the same interest in Iz, but I had a sense of why. Iz was outrageous and a magnet for drama, which had probably put Julia off. She'd had enough drama in Brooklyn.

I almost felt like I was cheating on Iz, although I realized how ridiculous that was. I shouldn't have to include her in *everything*. A little distance was healthy, especially since I was going away to college.

Julia pulled the cord to get off the bus and we stepped onto a busy block downtown. I spotted a weathered sign that said "The Ring," and followed her through a heavy door.

The massive room looked like a converted warehouse. There were two boxing rings on either side of the space and separate areas for sparring, punching bags, and weight training. The sounds of grunting and cheering echoed across the room.

I smiled. "Yeah, I'm safe here."

"There's Eric." Julia pointed toward the weight training section. He was doing some bench presses, with a massive guy spotting him.

"Let's not bug him until he's finished a few sets," Julia said. "He says I distract him."

"I'm sure that's a compliment."

She actually blushed. "Hey, look who's pummeling someone in the ring. That's Ortiz in the red shorts."

Ortiz. I couldn't see his face because of the headgear, but I could see the tall, muscled body glistening with sweat. Too bad my girls were missing it.

"It's okay to drool," Julia said.

"I wasn't drooling. I was admiring his shiny shorts."

She smirked. "He might've run out on you like a jackass, but he was into you. That's why I brought you over to him in the first place."

"What made you think he was into me?"

"He told Eric he saw you at the store sometimes. Said you were hot."

"He said that?"

"Absolutely."

Wow.

Double wow.

"Then why didn't he ask for my number?" I sighed. "Iz could be right. He could have a girlfriend. Or a string of them."

"Maybe he's a gigolo who answers booty calls for female executives."

I smirked. But as I watched him beat down his opponent, my mouth went dry. "There's not enough cash in the world to pay for a piece like that." I winked at her, and we burst out laughing.

When Eric had finished his last set, we went up to him. He smiled when he saw his girlfriend. "Hey, Divine." It was a play on her last name, DiVino. Eric wrapped his sweaty self around her, and she didn't seem to mind one bit.

"Maddie, how's it going?" he asked me once Julia had slipped out of his arms.

"Good. Just scoping the place out, seeing if it's a good place to train."

"The cat-fighting gym's down the street," he said. Julia punched his arm. "I was playin'!"

"He is *so* not PC," Julia said.

Eric drank some water, wiped his mouth, and checked the clock. "I'm going up for the sparring circle. Wanna watch?"

We agreed and followed him up some metal stairs to the loft. It was a big empty space with blue mats on the floor. There were four guys up there, stretching and air-boxing. Eric skipped a little rope to warm up. I didn't know what a sparring circle was, but I doubted it involved holding hands and singing.

Julia and I stood against the wall as the guys assembled into a circle. "I hate this," she said into my ear. "But he likes it when I watch."

"That sounds so wrong, you know," I teased.

"Trust me, I know."

The last guy to join them was Ortiz. He walked by without noticing us and took his place in the circle. Once everybody was quiet, he pointed at Eric, and then another guy. "You and you. Go."

It didn't look like boxing to me. It was street fighting, fast and dirty. Julia chewed her lip, wincing every time Eric *or* his opponent landed a kick or a punch. I didn't like it either. I knew that a lot of guys had a natural fighting urge in them, an instinct left over from our primitive selves. *Feeding the beast*, Ortiz had called it that night at Eric's party. But I guess it was better to control it in a boxing gym than to let it loose in a bar brawl.

The fight went on for two, maybe three minutes, but I could tell that for Julia, it felt like hours. Eric's opponent finally tapped out, admitting defeat.

Next Eric called the pair. He chose Ortiz and a bear of a guy who must've outweighed him by fifty pounds. It didn't matter. Ortiz stunned him with several rapid-fire punches, then pinned him to the ground. Obviously Ortiz wasn't just a studied fighter, he was a born one. Strange, because the Corner Store Guy I'd seen so many times didn't give off an air of aggression. Sex appeal, sure, but not aggression.

The sparring circle lasted about twenty minutes. By the end of it, the guys looked exhausted, and Julia did too.

Afterward Eric came up to us and downed some more water. "We going somewhere?"

Julia turned to me. "You up for it?"

"Nah, I'd better get home and work."

"Come on," Eric said, "they can't take away your scholarship now, can they?"

"It's the school newspaper. If the articles suck, it's on me. Great seeing you guys."

Out of the corner of my eye I could see Ortiz heading in

our direction. After the quick end to our last meeting, I knew it would be awkward to stand around and chat with him. I decided to make a strategic exit.

The bus stop was only steps from the front door of the gym. According to my iPhone app, I had to wait seven minutes, and the bus ride back would be twenty. Not bad. I could be at my computer by nine thirty, hopefully in bed by eleven.

I checked my phone and saw a text from Iz.

> What are we doing tomorrow night? Carmen says she's busy Friday AND Saturday night with Rafael. Can you believe that?

Actually I could. Carmen hadn't been returning my texts lately. She seemed to be making a point of showing us how into Rafael she was. I texted Iz back.

> Maybe we shouldn't have made fun of her Eric obsession.

Her reply came within two minutes.

> If she hadn't talked so much about him we wouldn't have. Whatevs!

A horn honked, and I looked up. A black car had stopped at the curb. Ortiz was in the driver's seat, his hair and skin glistening from a shower. I blinked. Must've been the quickest shower known to man. Did he deliberately hurry up so he could drive me?

"Why don't you get in? I'm going to work."

The car behind him beeped, jolting me. I hurried up to his car and slipped into the passenger seat. "Thanks."

The second I buckled my seat belt, he started to drive. "I'm guessing you live near Sasso's."

"Yeah, I'm just off Seventeenth."

After a couple of minutes, he said, "Not a boxing fan, are you?"

"What I saw up there wasn't exactly boxing."

"Yeah, it's more raw. Nothing's off-limits. That's how I like it."

Oh yeah? I was tempted to reply. But he looked so cool that I wasn't totally sure he was flirting with me. So I said, "I guess it's okay to fight like that if you're not training for competition."

"I'm not chasing the Rocky dream, trust me. But self-defense can come in handy."

That made me stop and think for a minute. "Were you there any of the times Sasso's was robbed?"

"Yeah, a few times."

"Really? Hope you weren't tempted to test out your skills."

He scoffed. "The sight of a gun kills the temptation to use my moves. Plus, any self-respecting stickup guy knows not to get within an arm's length of you."

"*Self-respecting* stickup guy? Seems like an oxymoron to me."

"Don't see why." He slanted me a look. "It's a trade like any other."

"Yeah, right. Aren't trades supposed to be *legal?*"

His mouth crooked. "Not in this city. You've got the drug trade. The gun trade. The sex trade."

"Okay, you got me there. But they're not like other trades—by the time you've been in five years, you're probably dead instead of a master tradesman."

"You got *me* there." He stopped at a light. His eyes drifted over me. I swallowed.

A tight silence settled over us. The cabin of the car suddenly seemed too small. I had a flash of my dream in which we were driving together, my hair blowing in the wind, my hand on his hard, muscled thigh.

Damn it. I shouldn't let my mind go there. Ortiz was sexy in a way that made my insides melt, and he undoubtedly knew it. Every hot-blooded female between fourteen and forty would be attracted to him. Maybe some cougars, too.

The point was, he could have any girl he wanted. If we

hooked up, it probably wouldn't go anywhere. And the last thing I needed was a booty call setup. Okay, so maybe I *needed* it, but I definitely shouldn't go for it.

Distracting myself, I turned to look out the window. Little bungalows and palm trees rushed by. I'd always loved my neighborhood. Not in an *I want to stay here forever* way but in a nostalgic way. I loved how my neighbors lived on their porches, how they all looked out for each other. Sure, I grew up knowing about the gangs, the violence, but none of it had ever touched my life. I'd always felt safe.

Until that night.

The moment I thought of Hector, I mentally pressed Delete. I'd taught myself to do that whenever the memory came up. Put it in a box and seal it with UPS tape and ship it off to Siberia. Compartmentalizing, Dr. Drew called it.

I called it staying sane.

Then I thought of Ortiz heading for another graveyard shift, and my stomach felt queasy. "I hope the graveyard shift's worth the risk."

"It's fine. Quiet. I can read, listen to my iPod. But as I told your friend, it takes real *stamina*."

He winked at me, and I couldn't help laughing.

The tension in the car had evaporated, but my house was coming up far too fast. I pointed to the right side of the street. "It's one eighty-six, second from the corner."

He pulled up to the curb and put the car in park.

"Thanks a lot," I said, unbuckling my seat belt and getting out. "Have a good night."

"You, too."

I shut the door on the seat belt. Classic move on my part. "Oops, sorry." I fumbled to put it back in, then shut the door again. His face stayed neutral, but I was pretty sure he was amused.

I hurried up to unlock my front door, not looking back until I was inside.

His car was still there, engine running. Sign of a gentleman, I thought with a smile.

THIEF

"I HAVE ANOTHER GUY FOR YOU," Iz declared the next morning when I parked my butt beside her on the bus. "I'll hook you up this weekend."

I sighed and sipped my coffee. The bus lurched, spilling the hot liquid on my jeans. This wasn't my day. I could feel it.

"It's okay, Iz," I grumbled. "I'm still not over Jack."

"Don't even joke about that. He thinks you're a total snob, you know."

I caught the edge in her voice. "What? You think he's right?"

"Not a *total* snob, no. But you obviously think you're too good for the guys I introduce you to."

"You've got to be kidding."

I wasn't in the mood for Iz's drama. I closed my eyes for a second, wishing I was back in bed. It wasn't homework that had kept me up late—it was my mind, which had replayed every second of the car ride with Ortiz.

"Wake up, Maddie. You can't go thinking you're better than everyone all the time. Guys don't go for that."

Ouch. I was used to Iz bitching at her boyfriends, not me. Did she actually believe that? Was this about the scholarship?

Before I could say anything, she gave a big sigh. "Sorry for being a bitch. But you should've at least given Jack a chance. I would have."

So that was what this was about. Iz kept trying to get me with guys that *she* would've gone for, and every time I passed one up, she took it personally.

"Look, Iz, it's super nice of you to try. But don't bother setting me up with another guy. I'm fine."

"You're *not* fine. You said last week you were horny as hell!"

A middle-aged woman in front of us turned with a look of disgust. My face went red.

Iz laughed. "It's true! Have you noticed how happy Carmen is right now? She says I'm a master matchmaker."

"Yeah, and she's ditching us this weekend to be with him. How'd that work out for you?"

"Okay, point for you. But at least she's not still going on

about Eric. I was ready to slap that girl sideways."

It was the perfect time to mention that I'd seen Eric and Julia last night, but I kept my mouth shut. Although I didn't want to keep anything from Iz, I didn't want to rub it in her face either. And she was being kinda clingy these days, more than usual. Must be because I was leaving in the fall.

Something clicked in my mind. Maybe *that* was why she wanted to find me a guy so badly. Because she wanted a reason for me to come back to Miami. Because she was afraid of losing me.

I might be moving away, but I wasn't going to let our friendship suffer. Maybe once she realized that, she'd stop sending all those guys my way.

My morning classes dragged. I spent lunch hour working on my article in the library, sneaking bites of a sandwich under the study carrel. I actually enjoyed writing about what to expect at college. I could fantasize about all the cool things ahead—making new friends in the dorms, partying during orientation week, choosing my classes, meeting my professors. But there were things to beware of too, like the pretty insane rates of sexual assault reported by freshmen girls. And then there were the health concerns. It turned out the "freshman fifteen" wasn't a myth, thanks to greasy cafeteria food.

I wanted to cut last period, but I wouldn't dare miss physics. Ms. Tate was going to give hints on the next test, which she always did on Friday afternoons to stop people from cutting. Contrary to what Eric thought, I could still lose my scholarship if my grades plummeted or if I failed a class.

On the bus home, Tom called to tell me there was a four o'clock staff meeting. I wished I hadn't answered it. I'd been so looking forward to a nap before work.

As I approached the house, I heard Dex barking in the backyard. There was a white van in the driveway.

I stayed on the sidewalk, not wanting to get closer to the house. I took out my phone to call Mom at the hotel. Then Boyd's heavy body stepped backward out the front door, holding our forty-inch flat screen TV.

"Boyd," I called out. "What are you doing?"

He went down the steps and headed right past me. "Picking up some of my stuff." When he got to the van, he set it down inside and wiped his forehead.

Bald and bearded, Boyd wasn't a good-looking man, and the gray sweatpants and stained T-shirt didn't help his cause. I still couldn't figure out how he'd scored a date with my mom in the first place.

I peeked into the back of the van. An end table, a tall mirror, a stack of DVDs. We had very little worth taking, and he was taking it. Of course, he hadn't bothered to load up his junk from the backyard.

I'd bugged Mom a million times to get our locks changed. I should've done it myself.

"Why are you taking our TV?"

"*Your* TV?" His eyelids disappeared with that oh-so-familiar glare. "Don't you remember it was a birthday gift?"

Yeah, right. Birthday gift. How convenient that he picks it up when he knows Mom won't be home. "I don't remember."

"That's a shame. Why don't you use your McDonald's money to buy a new one?"

I gritted my teeth. I so wanted to tell him off. But the sound of Dex barking in the backyard reminded me not to lose it. Until the divorce was final, Dex legally belonged to Boyd. I knew that he hated Dex for being disloyal, for choosing me over him. But I had no doubt that he'd take him back just to hurt us.

"Fucking dog never stops," Boyd said. "Tried to bite my hand off."

I wish he had.

"Is there anything else I can help you carry before I head to work?" I asked.

Boyd narrowed his eyes suspiciously. It was incredible that, even now, he couldn't read me. Couldn't smell how much I hated him.

"That's it for now," he said. "I'll be back another time for the stuff in the backyard."

"Okay, then. Take care." I turned my back on him and walked inside. Only then did I let the tears come.

I opened the patio door, and Dex shot in from the backyard. He was furious, jumping around, barking, nearly knocking me over. I tried to grab his collar, but he yanked away from me, circling the house twice before realizing that Boyd had left.

"Shhh. It's okay, he's gone." I noogied his neck and gave him a couple of treats, which got his tail wagging again.

I grabbed a Twix from Mom's guilty pleasure drawer in the kitchen, surveying the house. The living room looked bare without the TV and the end table. Mom was going to be really upset. I didn't want to ruin her day by calling her, so I left a note on the kitchen table.

Hey Mom.

As you can see, Boyd took a few things that he said were his. Let's just let it go. If we don't, he's gonna come for Dex. It's almost over, Mom!!!

Love you,
Maddie XOX

P.S. Let's have taquitos tonight when I get home?

I knew I should definitely stay home that night to be with Mom. She needed the support, and I wanted to make sure she didn't call up Boyd. Though I'd planned to watch a movie with Iz and Abby, they'd understand. They knew the deal with Boyd.

I gave Dex another treat and he nuzzled my hip. I closed my eyes. God, I loved him.

We were almost rid of Boyd.

Almost.

THE GANG

BY THE TIME I GOT TO WORK, the meeting had already started. Twenty employees were packed into the staff room, Ronald McDonald watching over them like a minister with his flock. I slipped to the back of the room, snagging a free chair beside Manny.

"Hey, Diaz," he whispered, passing me a handout labeled *Security Procedures.*

"Hey. Who's that?" I asked. A lady at the front of the room was doing a PowerPoint presentation. She wore high heels and a slick gray suit.

"Regional HQ. Security shit. A fight broke out at the Miller Drive McDonald's last night and two people got stabbed."

"Are they okay?"

"Don't know. There's a lot of shit happening in the neighborhood these days. You probably heard about it from your friends at Rivera."

"I haven't heard much this past week. What's going on?"

"More like, what *isn't* going on? It's fights, stickups, shakedowns, and that's just within two blocks of here. *And* there's a full moon this weekend."

"Lovely."

"HQ's worried that we'll lose business. They're gonna do some things to make it look like we're a safe place for families to eat."

"*Look* like we're safe?"

He shrugged. "They're talking about bulletproof glass at the drive-through. But other than that, we can't exactly have a buzzer at the door. Gangbangers are half our business."

"And we have the security cameras," I said. But cameras hadn't stopped Sasso's from being robbed, so I doubted they'd prevent trouble here.

"Tom wants a panic button, too."

A panic button? I knew that our McDonald's wasn't the safest place on earth, but this was extreme. What if some Reyes decided to come and pay me a visit? I was a sitting duck.

As if he could read my mind, Manny said, "Don't you go worrying, Diaz. You're safe here. Anyone gets near you, I'll deep-fry his ass."

When the meeting ended, I took my place at the back and got to work. But I was on edge, and the kick of caffeine from my McCafé latte only made me more jittery. It must've been an awful scene at the Miller Drive McDonald's when the fight broke out. I hoped nothing like that ever happened here.

The Friday dinner rush ebbed a bit early, which gave me too much time to think. Mom was probably home by now, freaking out over Boyd's theft. I just hoped my note stopped her from doing something stupid.

My phone vibrated—it was a text from Iz saying that she and Abby were going to repaint her room (for the seventeenth time). The theme was Evening Stars, she said, and everybody was gonna "go Lady Gaga over it."

On break, I checked my phone again, and saw that Iz had already posted the *Before* bedroom pictures on Facebook. I "liked" it immediately. Then I ate a small salad, which would keep me until Mom's taquitos later.

Manny came in and sat down across from me. "What are our plans later, Diaz? A movie? Romantic walk on the beach?"

"Taquitos with my mom. I'm staying home tonight."

"How's Isa-Dora the Explorer taking it?"

"She's painting her room." I showed him a picture on my phone. "What are *you* doing later, Manny? Cruising the bars? Trolling the streets for girls?"

He smirked. "Actually, I'm gonna study."

"Study? For what?"

"Heating and cooling."

That took me by surprise. "I didn't know you were in school."

"Just part-time for now. In the fall I'll start my apprenticeship full-time. Bye-bye, Micky D's." He eyed me. "What, you thought this was my career?"

I shrugged, a little embarrassed. "I wasn't sure what your plan was."

A knowing smile. "See, we're more alike than you think, Diaz. You got your plans, and I got mine. I'm an ambitious man, mamacita." He snapped his fingers. "And I've got just what you need."

"Good to know, Manny. I'll keep it in mind."

The second latte was a mistake. As I waited for the bus after work, my whole body buzzed with caffeine. Or maybe it was my usual paranoia. Although I stood at the bus stop with several people, I didn't feel safe.

I heard a rustle behind me and practically jumped out of my skin. The heavyset woman next to me started at my reaction, pressing a hand to her large chest.

"Sorry," I said. I hoped she didn't have a heart condition. It was probably just a cat in the bushes. Or a squirrel. Or a freaking ant.

I needed a distraction. I glanced down at my phone. Iz had posted more pictures of her bedroom makeover. In each one, she and Abby were posing. One shot caught Iz midair, leaping off the bed in tiny shorts and an even tinier tank top. I smiled and shook my head.

The squeal of tires brought my head up. In the same second, someone hooked my neck with his arm, slamming me to the pavement. As I fell, the world streaked red before my eyes. Then they were on me.

Two guys. Maybe three. I couldn't see. I'd squeezed my eyes shut against the blows raining down on me.

Adrenaline coursed through me. I fought with every bit of strength I had. Tried to enlist my arms to protect my head, but they smashed right through them.

A kick to my ribs. Pain curled me up.

I knew this was coming, I realized. I knew it the moment I'd looked through the one-way mirror and identified Hector's killers. It didn't matter how many times I'd told myself that the Reyes wouldn't come after me.

I knew there'd be payback.

I couldn't scream. There was screaming around me, female screaming, but it wasn't mine. I heard people calling for help. *It's not enough*, I wanted to shout at them. *Why can't you help me?*

Because they're scared. Like I was scared the night the Reyes had set Hector on fire.

A blow smacked my head into the pavement. The shock reverberated through my skull. I felt myself shrinking away, retreating to the safety of the darkness. But I forced myself not to let go. If I lost consciousness, I wouldn't be able to resist them anymore. And I might never wake up.

Somewhere in the quiet part of my mind, I recognized that, back at home, Mom was making me taquitos. And that I would never be home to eat them.

The blows suddenly stopped. I opened my eyes long enough to see my worst nightmare: they were pulling me toward a car. New panic sent a jolt through me, and I struggled wildly, trying to dislodge myself from their arms. But it got me nowhere. I went dead weight. One of them lost his grip on my left arm, and I twisted, slamming a fist into his groin. But I couldn't shake the other one.

Someone rammed into us, and I was flung to the ground. I put my hands over my head, bracing for what came next, but nothing did. I glanced up, my vision swimming into focus. There were guys fighting around me, punching and smashing each other.

Tires squealed, and the car sped away.

Two guys were beside me now. The blue-eyed one said, "It's okay."

He lifted me up. The tops of trees volleyed above me, bouncing around my vision. I felt the warm, metallic taste of blood in my mouth and nose. I tipped myself forward over his shoulder so I could breathe. Every part of me vibrated with pain.

But I was alive.

"It's okay," he repeated, walking fast. "We're helping you."

Instinctively, I knew that. These guys had done what no one else had—what I hadn't done for Hector. They'd intervened before it was too late.

We stopped moving. We were somewhere dark, maybe an alley. I must've blacked out for a few minutes, because I woke up in a moving car.

Voices.

"Two minutes, Lobo. How we gonna do this?" a guy shouted from the front seat.

"Stay put. I'll carry her in." The voice came from above me. I realized that my head was being cradled in someone's lap.

I looked up at him. He wore a black bandanna over his face. That couldn't be a good thing—I should be scared of him, shouldn't I? But I wasn't. I knew that I was safe. I felt it in the gentle way he was supporting my head.

"She's waking up," he said, his voice muffled by the bandanna. Then he looked down at me, guiding a lock of hair out of my eyes. "Helluva night, huh? Don't worry. You're gonna be fine."

Fine? There were pain receptors in a hundred parts of my body that wanted to argue. I was about to tell him, but when I took a breath, my rib cage pulled tight, and only a grunt came out.

"We're going to drop you off at the hospital, Madeleina."

The journalist in me wanted to pounce on that. How did he know my name? And why was he covering his face? Who was he?

The car glided to a stop, and a door opened. Then he swept me into the dizzying bright lights of the hospital. I felt him gently place me on a gurney.

He came face to face with a terrified nurse. "What's going on? Security! We need security over here!"

"Her name is Maddie Diaz," he said from behind his bandanna. "Take care of her." He bent to my ear. *"Hasta luego."*

Then he was gone.

NOT EVER

I WOKE UP TO THE SOUND OF A TOILET FLUSHING. When I opened my eyes, I saw Mom emerging from the bathroom. She was settling back in an orange plastic chair when she noticed I was awake. "Sorry, honey. Did I wake you?"

"What time is it?" My voice came out rough, like sandpaper.

She looked at her watch. "Just after three. You can go back to sleep if you want. I made the nurses promise not to disturb you until dinnertime."

"It's okay. I want to wake up." Easier said than done, considering the drugs I was on. I glanced at the IV bag attached to my arm. Whatever was in there spelled sweet relief.

I didn't have to ask Mom what my injuries were—I'd

learned all of that last night. The doctors and nurses had descended on me, assessing my injuries, and sending me for X-rays, stitches, and the rest. After several hours, they'd concluded that I had two broken ribs, a fractured arm, and a moderate concussion, not to mention gashes and bruises everywhere. Or, in the words of my rescuer, *You're gonna be fine.*

Lobo. That was the name he'd answered to. But why the name, and why hide his identity?

"Can you help me sit up?" I asked Mom. I'd had enough of lying flat.

Mom pressed a button on the bed and slowly eased me into a sitting position. That's when Iz came in, carrying a teddy bear from the gift shop.

"Maddie, you're awake! I thought you were gonna sleep *all* day." Iz pasted a big smile on her face, but her eyes were slightly red, and her mascara had left dark smudges beneath her eyes. "Here, this is for you."

She handed me a little pink bear with GET WELL on his chest. "Aw, cute."

"Better be, for twenty bucks," Iz said, a hand going to her hip. "That place is a total rip-off. So, you all healed up? I thought we'd cruise the waiting room downstairs. I must've seen a dozen guys with surfing-related injuries."

"Soon as I can." My whole face tightened as I tried to smile, and I felt a bandage pull at my hairline.

Iz turned to my mom. "I saw a few hot doctors who weren't wearing wedding rings."

"I'll expect you to get me some phone numbers, Iz," Mom said. But she didn't have Iz's talent for pretended cheer. It occurred to me that Mom was still wearing her pajamas. Not everyone would know it, since she was wearing sweatpants and an old T-shirt. She must have gotten a call last night and been at the hospital ever since.

"Are you hungry?" Mom asked. "Let me see if I can get you a sandwich or something."

Iz reached for the hospital phone. "I'll call someone."

"There's no room service," I said, suddenly wanting to laugh. My chest bucked, like a hiccup, causing a jolt of pain.

"Are you okay?" Mom and Iz asked at once.

"I'm fine. Anyway, I'm not hungry." Seeing the worry in my mom's eyes, I said, "But I'm sure I will be soon. Hey, Iz, tell us more about the hot doctors."

Called to action, Iz sat down and started to talk. I watched Mom, hoping Iz was distracting her. But I didn't think so. There was a stark sadness in her eyes that reminded me of a lost child. I'd seen that expression once before, in the terrible weeks after Dad had died.

Someone knocked, but before we could answer it, the door opened. Detective Gutierrez came in with a female officer in uniform.

"Hello, Maddie. How are you feeling?" Detective Gutierrez approached me.

"No!" Mom bolted out of her chair, putting herself between the cops and my bed. "I told the staff to keep you out of here."

The cops exchanged a *she's crazy* look. Detective Gutierrez put his hands together in a peace gesture. "I'm so sorry for what you've been through, Mrs. Diaz. I can't imagine. I just wanted to ask your daughter a couple of questions so we can find the people responsible for this."

Mom's eyes bulged. She got in his face, her index finger inches from his eyes. *"You* are responsible for this. They wouldn't have come after her if you hadn't pressured her to identify those gang members. Did you warn her of the risks? Or did you offer to protect her once she agreed to talk? Did you?"

His mouth flattened. "I'm doing my job, Mrs. Diaz. Your daughter did the right thing, and I'm very sorry that—"

"Get out of here, both of you!" Mom cried.

"Mom, stop," I said, worried she'd actually slap him.

She ignored me. "Stay the hell away from my daughter, or I'm calling my lawyer."

Detective Gutierrez nodded. "All right, Mrs. Diaz. We understand."

When the cops left the room, Mom collapsed into a chair and sobbed. Iz went over and put her arms around her. I tried to get out of bed to do the same, but my body protested. This was all my fault. I'd put my mom through this because I'd chosen to testify. Because of *my* decision, she'd almost lost the only person she had left.

Mom was right about one thing—I *had* been pressured to testify. But that wasn't why I'd done it. I'd done it for Hector. I had failed him that night in the park, but I could stand up for him now. And as much as I regretted hurting my mom so much, I couldn't regret my decision to identify Hector's killers.

Not now, not ever.

Mom wouldn't budge from the hospital until I ate something. I made a show of eating half a tuna sandwich and drinking some milk. Then Mom said she didn't want me to be alone. Iz promised her she'd stay with me until I fell asleep. Finally, Mom agreed to go.

The moment Mom left the room, Iz heaved a sigh. I could tell she was just as relieved as I was. I could also tell that she was done with the fluff talk. "What happened last night, Maddie? Do you even remember?"

"Yeah, I do." I'd once heard that if a memory is too traumatic, the human mind will block it out. It will hide it away in your subconscious until you choose to dig it up. But I recalled last night's attack in vivid technicolor, down to the smallest details—the scratchy whiskers on the chin of one of my attackers, something sharp under my back, the voices calling for help. I remembered other things too—like Lobo's gentle touch, and the kind words he'd spoken to me.

"It was the Reyes, wasn't it?" Iz asked, searching my eyes.

I nodded. "They didn't stop to identify themselves. But yeah."

"When I walked by this morning, there was blood on the sidewalk." Iz blinked back some tears. "Your friend Manny's been texting me all day. I don't know how the hell he got my number, but he's a pain in the ass. He blames himself for not waiting at the bus stop with you."

That was Manny. "Tell him it's not his fault. I was at a crowded bus stop, for God's sake. He couldn't have predicted what would happen."

"No kidding." She paused, taking a breath. "I heard some guys, like, saved your life and brought you to the hospital."

"Yeah. They stopped the Reyes from pushing me into a car." I closed my eyes, remembering the horrible feeling when I'd known they were going to take me. "If the Reyes had gotten me into that car, I wouldn't be here right now."

It felt strange to say it out loud. But the truth was, the guys who had attacked me hadn't planned to scare me—they had planned to kill me. To make sure I couldn't testify against

Ramon and Diego. I knew it in my gut.

"Who were the guys who helped you?" Iz asked. "They definitely deserve a fruit basket. Or a fucking lap dance from the hottest bitches in town."

"I didn't know them. One of them had this nickname: Lobo. And he knew my name, which was kind of weird."

"Lobo?" Her eyes widened. "Fuck. Me. You're kidding."

"What? You know him?"

"Know him? Lobo is the leader of the Destinos, the gang that's been screwing with the Reyes."

I stared at her. *The Destinos?*

It was unbelievable.

I'd been rescued by the gang everybody was talking about. And I'd had no clue.

Was that why the Destinos had saved me—because their goal was to mess with the Reyes? No way, it wasn't just business. Lobo's kindness hadn't been faked.

"It makes sense," I said. "Lobo kept his face covered, even in the car. It seemed really important to him to keep his identity secret."

"Important? Salazar would cut off his right ball to find out who Lobo is! Everybody says that Lobo figures out Salazar's next move before he knows it himself. It's burning Salazar's ass. It's like Lobo's some sort of superspy—or even psychic."

Psychic? It seemed far-fetched, but there was something

different about him, almost mystical.

"Now I understand why they didn't stay with me and wait for an ambulance," I said. "The Destinos wouldn't want to be identified. And if they'd left me at the scene, the Reyes might've come back to finish the job."

Iz was all wound up. "Shit, Maddie, I can't believe the Destinos saved you! That is so badass. Now think. What was Lobo like? Was he tall or short? How old was he?"

"I have no idea. I never got a clear look at him."

"Okay, but do you think he was good-looking? I know his face was covered, but good-looking guys have this sexy vibe. You know what I'm saying?"

Iz was over the top, and I loved her for it. "Okay, fine, there *was* something sexy about him. I can't explain it."

"Quadruple freaking wow. Of course he was sexy. It's the power, Maddie. He's got Salazar looking for him twenty-four/seven, which would scare most people shitless, but not Lobo. He just keeps going. And *that*'s sexy as hell. Even if he's got a face full of craters and bulldog lips. Power is sexy."

I doubted his face fit that description. All I knew for sure was that I was dying to see him again. When he had dropped me off at the hospital, he'd said, "*Hasta luego.*" *Until the next time.*

I hoped he'd meant it.

THE VISITOR

I FELL ASLEEP LISTENING TO BALLADS ON IZ'S IPOD. In my dream I roamed the streets of Miami, which had become a postapocalyptic wasteland. I was alone, a crossbow strapped to my back. Humans with no eyes would step out in front of me, and I shot them down, one by one. I felt powerful, almost invincible. And then my eyes flicked open and I saw myself in the hospital bed. The powerful feeling dissolved.

I fell into another dream immediately. A jumble of images of my childhood flashed before me like snapshots in a camera commercial. I saw my dad and grandparents smiling, joking around. I saw myself crying over a toy my cousin had taken from me. I saw days at the beach, sandy toes, and sunburn peeling off my shoulders.

When I surfaced from the dream, I was aware that someone had come into my room. I opened my eyes, expecting to find a nurse checking my IV or getting ready to replace a bandage.

But it was him.

He was standing by my bed, as still as silence. He wore a black bandanna over his face and a black cap tucked low over his eyes. I wasn't afraid. I knew that he was the one who'd cradled my head in his lap and stroked my hair.

"I had to see you," he said.

My chest filled with every emotion. "Lobo."

"You know who I am." He didn't sound happy.

"That name doesn't tell me who you are."

"It tells you enough. More than you need to know."

"I don't know anything. I think you're probably a dream. Are you?"

He shook his head. "I'm blood and bone, like you, Madeleina. I want you to know that you're safe now. The Reyes who attacked you won't come after you again. And neither will the others."

My mind wrapped around that slowly. "How can you know that?"

"You just have to trust me."

"Did you kill the guys who attacked me?" I looked up at the black bandanna, wishing I could see through it. Wishing I could at least see the expression in his shaded eyes.

"No, I didn't kill them. But they deserved to die for what they did to you. And for what they would have done."

His words sent a chill through me. We both knew what he meant.

"I want to know who you are, Lobo."

He gave a shrug. "I'm the one who's looking out for you. Nothing else matters."

I'm the one who's looking out for you. Something was beginning to dawn on me. "You had people follow me, didn't you? Is that why they were there when I got attacked?"

"Yes. My guys were following you."

So my instincts had been right. I *was* being followed. But I still didn't understand why he'd have them look out for me.

"I know you have questions," he said. "But the answers won't free you from all of this. That's what you want, isn't it?"

He was right. I wanted to be free of this whole nightmare. I wanted to move on with my life.

Lobo took a step forward, his black jeans coming in contact with the bed rail. He traced a finger along the side of my face. His touch was gentle, and his energy buzzed through me. I could feel it course through my blood and hum in my ears.

I lifted my arm, anchored by the IV, and took his hand. He was so close, I held my breath. It felt like everything in the room—everything in the world—stilled.

Although his hand was much bigger than mine, our hands fit perfectly together. And if I had my way, he would never let go.

The moment I had the thought, I felt his grip slip from mine. He moved away from the bed.

"Sleep now, Madeleina."

The click of the door told me he had left the room. I wanted to call him back, to keep him beside me. I felt safe with him next to me.

Lobo had saved my life. He'd had his guys follow me, a girl he didn't even know. I owed him. I owed him everything. But how could I repay him if I didn't know who he was?

And then it hit me that I'd forgotten to thank him.

In the morning, I was discharged from the hospital. I spent the next few days horizontal. Sometimes I lay on a lounger in the backyard, soaking in the April sun while Dex dug holes in the lawn. I would close my eyes and pretend I was on vacation until an aching part of my body set me straight.

I couldn't resist the temptation to watch news stories about my attack and scour the online newspapers.

WITNESS TO HOMELESS MURDER ASSAULTED.
BRUTAL ATTACK ON KEY WITNESS.

The headlines were splashy, but the journalism was shitty—even a high school newspaper editor like me could see that. And the timeline was usually way off. Some news sources placed the attack as early as seven p.m., others as late as midnight.

I felt an odd detachment from it all. Since I was a minor, my name was never used—I was just "the witness," which allowed me to pretend it wasn't me. I got plenty of calls from news agencies; I gave them nothing. But Roz Wilson, the heavyset woman who'd been standing beside me at the bus stop, was all too eager to talk. I admit, I couldn't help but like Roz. She had a talent for over-the-top descriptions. In an interview with KTU Local 5, she managed to use "horrid," "horrific," and "horrifying" all in one thirty-second sound bite.

My recovery was slow but steady. I ached less every day, which meant fewer meds and a clearer head. By Wednesday I was able to work on my laptop, and I dove into both newspaper and school work. My goal was to return to school on Monday, no matter what.

My Facebook page blew up with sympathy posts. I spent endless time scrolling through them, assuring people that I was okay. Then Iz called me up, ranting that I should *not*, under any circumstances, downplay my injuries in case they ever caught the guys who did this to me.

Fat chance of that. I hadn't seen my attackers clearly enough to identify them. And even if I could, more Reyes would probably come after me.

Not according to Lobo, I reminded myself.

I still didn't understand how that could be true. But at the same time, I didn't doubt him. I'd felt something that night in the hospital when we'd held hands, some intense emotion I couldn't identify, but wanted desperately to feel again. My intuition told me that he would come back to me, somehow— that I couldn't possibly have seen the last of him. It was only a question of when.

There were other visitors, though. My friends stopped in to see me often. And Manny sent me flirty text messages to keep me entertained. It all helped. But it was Julia who helped me the most. She'd been through her own nightmare back in Brooklyn, and she understood me like no one else.

She stopped in to see me on Tuesday, and again on Friday before her four o'clock class. We sat in the living room and drank cans of iced tea. She didn't have to ask how I was doing. She saw.

"Emotional day, huh?"

I felt a lump in my throat. "I looked up Hector Rodriguez last night and found his sister's Facebook page. She's a real estate agent with three kids. She wrote about what a good brother he was, and his struggle with mental illness."

"Must've made him more real to you."

I nodded. "I read some more articles about his murder and they made me so angry. They kept calling him 'the homeless man' and hardly mentioned his name. Like he wasn't even a person."

"That's what the press does. It's just like when they say a murder's 'gang-related.' It means regular people don't have to worry about it."

"I keep thinking how lucky I am that those guys intervened." Although I wanted to tell her that "those guys" were the Destinos, I knew I had to keep it quiet. "I should've done the same for Hector. But I was too scared."

Julia shook her head firmly. "Don't do that, Maddie. You're going to drive yourself crazy."

"I know. But during the attack, I kept wanting someone to help me. Hector must have been thinking the same thing."

"There's no comparison. You wouldn't have stood a chance."

"What if I'd been able to distract them? It could've played out differently."

"You couldn't have saved Hector. You have to accept that. If you'd approached them, they would've raped you and set *you* on fire instead. Your gut told you to stay away, and you followed it."

I closed my eyes, taking it in. I so wanted to believe her.

"But you're helping Hector now, and you're paying the

price. Look at you, for God's sake."

Yeah, look at me. I was a complete mess.

"I've been there, Maddie," she said, her tone softening. "When I got jumped, I looked just as bad as you—and it sucked. But at least your friends are standing by you. Mine didn't."

I couldn't imagine that. "How did you get through it?"

"Eric. He was my rock. We got through the shitstorm and were stronger for it. It might sound hokey, but I'm one of those *everything happens for a reason* people."

"I like those people." I wished I could be one. It would be a relief to think that everything happened the way it was meant to. It would mean I didn't have to feel regret or wonder *what if.*

Although Julia's words were comforting, I still saw myself as a coward. I'd never know what would've happened if I'd intervened to help Hector—and I knew that would haunt me forever. All I could do was promise myself that if someone ever needed my help again, I would step up instead of cowering in the dark.

DOUBT

MONDAY MORNING I WENT BACK TO SCHOOL. According to Iz, I only appeared "a little banged-up." Which was a lot better than last week, when I'd looked "so Guantánamo."

At least she was honest. Most people made a point of saying how great I looked. I almost believed it until I came face-to-face with the purple-yellow bruises in my locker mirror.

Thankfully, the story of my attack had died out of the press in the last few days, and Roz Wilson's fifteen minutes had ended. But the latest headlines were a lot more disturbing. Three girls in their twenties had been found in a makeshift brothel in Kendall. They'd been drugged and abused. It turned out that the girls were illegal immigrants, brought into the country by sex traffickers. Maybe I'd write an article about it for the newspaper.

At lunch, I met with Ms. Halsall. She greeted me cheerfully, but her eyes were full of concern. "It's great to have you back, Maddie. You're looking well."

"Thanks." We sat down at two desks in the middle of the classroom. "How'd the meeting go last week?"

"Fine. Everybody's on task for the May edition." She pulled a stack of paper from her briefcase. "Thanks for sending all this. I really didn't expect you to get so much done while you were away. I've polished up the other articles, so we're ready for Parminder to do the layout. We can go to print on Friday."

"Thanks. That's a huge relief."

Her eyes were kind. "You've been through a lot the past few weeks, Maddie. Everyone's rooting for you. I was thinking it might be easiest if someone else took over the last two papers."

I straightened, causing pain to shoot through my ribs. "Are you serious?"

"You have so much on your plate already."

"Did you think I screwed up those articles? I know the sports section was a little confusing, but Josh was away with the soccer team, so I did the best I could to clean it up myself."

"You've done an excellent job. That's the thing, Maddie. I'm concerned you're working too hard." She smiled gently. "You have nothing to prove. Give yourself time to relax, to heal. To focus on wrapping up your classes. If you step down as editor, no one will think any less of you."

"Step down?" Ms. Halsall just didn't get it. How could she think it would help me to take away the most important thing in my life? I needed to be the editor of *Prep Talk*. Without it, I was just that girl who'd seen the homeless man murdered. The witness who'd been attacked. I *needed* to be someone other than that girl.

"No way. I don't want to step down. I know you're trying to help, but please don't. What I need is to focus on my work. To focus on what I'm good at."

She watched me for a long moment, then gave a nod. "Sure, Maddie. Whatever you feel is best."

I was tired of it—the sympathetic stares of my classmates, the supportive words of my teachers. I was still me, not some china doll that had shattered into a million pieces.

All I wanted was for things to be normal again.

I spent my lunch hours and evenings working my butt off to catch up on every single assignment I'd missed. I probably could've gotten out of some of them, but I didn't want special treatment. Besides, working my butt off was *my* normal.

By Thursday, I was caught up. But I wasn't going to take a night off—I'd just end up thinking too much. So I started to research my new article on sex trafficking. I figured the topic was worth another look, especially because of this week's headlines. Once I showed it to Ms. Halsall, she'd be sorry she ever doubted me.

But as I did the research, I got choked up. The more details that came out, the more horrific the story was. The three Honduran girls had signed up to be au pairs in the United States, hoping to one day become landed immigrants. Those girls were just like me—they had big dreams, and they wanted something better than the life they knew.

I can't do this, I realized, closing the window on the latest website. All I could think of was how terrible this world was. How humans could be so cruel to one another. A flash of Hector came up, of his death struggle, and tears flooded my eyes.

No matter what I did, that night kept coming back. *Hector* kept coming back. A ghost in life because of his mental illness and addiction, a ghost in death because the papers refused to humanize him, to call him by name. He deserved more than that.

If I had been the one writing those newspaper articles, I would've written about his life, not just his death. I would've described the Hector Rodriguez his sister had written about on her Facebook page, not just the one who had died violently in the park.

Then it hit me: maybe I *could.*

I'd write a letter to the editor of the *Miami Herald*. But I'd have to do it anonymously. The last thing I needed was for the press to find out that the key witness was writing a tribute to Hector.

Damn, I was gonna do this.

I opened a new Word file and typed an opening paragraph.

On the night of March 20th, a homeless man was senselessly murdered in Emery Park. You've heard about it. And you've heard about the epidemic of gang violence, the plight of the homeless. But one thing is missing from all these stories: Hector Rodriguez himself.

You know the story of his death, but what about his life? Doesn't he deserve to have his story told?

I read it aloud. Good, but not good enough. It had to be the perfect opening or no one would bother to read on.

I reworked it several times, but it still wasn't quite right. So I switched gears and did some brainstorming on how to proceed. I decided to get some quotes from people who knew Hector. I could ask Ortiz, for starters. He'd said at the party that Hector was his most polite customer.

A while later, a text from Julia appeared.

Julia: What you up to, girl?

Maddie: Working on an article. You?

Julia: Watching Eric and Ortiz box. Ortiz is a madman tonight. Lots of pent-up sexual energy. I thought of you.

Maddie: Why me?

Julia: Because Ortiz asks Eric about you like every day.

Maddie: You're joking.

Julia: I'm not! He heard what happened to you and has been bugging Eric ever since. I told Eric to stop giving him updates and tell him to call you himself. We're going for a drink with him later. Wanna come?

Maddie: No way. He'd think it was a setup.

Julia: Oh come on. Who cares what he thinks? You need to get out, girl. We'll be at Louis's patio in half an hour.

Maddie: Fine. If you say so. ;)

Julia was right—I needed to get out. Besides, this was the perfect chance to get a quote from Ortiz for my article about Hector.

I changed into a fresh pair of jeans and a cute yellow muscle tee. I put on some makeup, playing up my eyes and lips, but my final look in the mirror made me cringe. My cheeks were still bruised, similar to when I'd had my wisdom teeth out, and I had a crusty red scab on my forehead where stitches had been removed. Did I really want Ortiz to see me like this?

Screw it.

An hour later, on the crowded patio of Louis's Bar and Grill, I knew I'd made the right decision. It was beautiful out. The sun had dipped low beneath the clouds, shining light crystals across the ocean. We were all laughing and eating appetizers while Julia told a story about her crazy teachers back in Brooklyn.

Ortiz sat next to me. Out of the corner of my eye, I saw him looking my way more often than he needed to. I tugged a lock of hair over my face self-consciously, hoping he wasn't staring at my bruises. At one point, I dared to glance back at him, and he flashed a smile that made my toes tingle.

I remembered something Iz had once told me: *The world needs more gorgeous guys*. At the time, I'd laughed it off. But now, I decided she was right. I wondered if Ortiz could actually see past my banged-up face, or if he was just being nice. It didn't matter—a little meaningless flirtation was good for me. Hell,

I'd take anything that boosted my spirits and didn't involve illegal drugs.

"This calamari is overcooked," Eric said, though he didn't stop eating it. "Rubbery, not tender. Chef Belanger would never allow this out of his kitchen."

He fed one to Julia. She shrugged. "I've never tasted calamari that isn't rubbery." She turned to Ortiz and me. "Eric's a big food critic these days. I keep telling him to start a blog."

"Fine with me, Divine," Eric said, mischief in his eyes. "I'll do the eating, you can do the writing."

Julia raised her brows. "Sounds like a raw deal to me. You should really start a blog about what it's like to work under a French chef."

"Diarie of a keetchen beetch," Eric said in a fake French accent.

"How much longer do you think you'll work there?" Ortiz asked him.

"I finish my course work in June, then I'll work there full time until Chef Belanger promotes me or fires me. He's an evil genius, yeah, but he's the real deal."

"I'd give it another year before you crack and strangle the man," Julia said.

Eric's mouth curved in a grin. "That's a possibility too." He looked at Ortiz. "What about you? You survive the Krav Maga course?"

Ortiz nodded. "Survived with all soft tissues intact."

"Huh?" Julia said, and we looked at each other in confusion. "What's this Krav stuff?"

"It's an Israeli fighting style," Ortiz said, taking a sip of Corona. "Picture boxing and jujitsu multiplied by ten. Instead of avoiding a person's weak spots, you target them."

"It's *real* fighting instead of sport fighting," Eric said. Before Julia could say anything, he put up his hands. "Don't worry, I'm not going to do it. It's hard-core even for me."

"Good. I need your weak spots intact, honey."

We all laughed. Eric smiled at her, and she smiled back. Then he pulled his chair against hers and hugged her close.

It was just a hug, not some big tongue kiss like Iz bestowed on her boyfriends, but I felt a prickle of . . . discomfort? Jealousy? Eric and Julia were *that* couple—the couple that reminded you of what they had and you didn't. Of what you might never be lucky enough to have. And yet they were such awesome people that you couldn't resent them for it.

I wondered if Ortiz was uncomfortable too. He turned to me. "What about your newspaper writing, Maddie? Still digging into Miami's underbelly?"

It was cool that he remembered. "I'm working on a new article. I'm hoping I can get it into one of the local papers as a letter to the editor. It's about Hector Rodriguez."

Ortiz raised an eyebrow. "Are you sure you should write

about him when you're testifying at his trial? I'd check with the cops on that one."

"I wouldn't publish it under my name. And it would be about his life, not his death."

"Oh. That's cool, then."

"I was thinking I'd interview a few neighborhood people who knew him. Thought you could give me a quote."

"Sure. Give me your number and I'll text it to you later."

I told him my number and he plugged it into his phone.

Julia and Eric had come back to reality and were watching us. I caught Julia's knowing look, and gave my head a subtle shake. Ortiz might have my phone number now, but other than sending me the quote for Hector, I doubted he would use it.

And it didn't matter. Ortiz was cool, but there was someone else on my mind now. Someone who'd been there when I'd needed him. Someone whose face I'd never seen, but who I was drawn to in a way I'd never thought possible.

I needed Lobo to come see me again. Soon.

LOBO

WHEN I WALKED INTO MCDONALD'S THE NEXT DAY after school, my coworkers went quiet. Stared. Whispered to each other.

Well, except for Manny. The moment he saw me, he came over and hugged me tight.

"God, Diaz," he said against my hair. "You scared the fuck out of me."

It felt good to have his arms around me. Safe. But since everybody was staring, I pulled away with a "Burger biatch is in da house."

I said a quick hi to everyone then went into the staff room. Manny followed me in. For once, he seemed tongue-tied. "You look better than I pictured."

"What kind of a compliment is that? Forget it—I'll take

it." I tossed my bag into a locker. "Your texts helped, Manny. Thanks. Iz wanted me to pass on a message to you: if you text her one more time for an update on my health, she'll kick your ass."

He actually blushed. "I didn't want to bug you too much. Listen, Diaz. I wanted to tell you this in person." He came up to me, stepping into my personal space. "I'm sorry I wasn't there to help you that night. I can't tell you how sorry."

"Why should you be sorry? You couldn't have known what was coming."

"I feel like shit that I downplayed the threat when you asked about the Reyes. I pride myself on keeping my ear to the ground, you know?" He looked like he was about to say more, but suddenly broke off. "I honestly didn't think they'd come after you."

"Don't worry about it. It's over now."

"Is it?" He searched my eyes, as if he didn't believe me.

His vulnerability tugged at my heart. I didn't know what I'd done for Manny to care about me like this. I didn't deserve it.

"As you can see, I'm fine. No thanks to your obscene text messages—they made me laugh so hard I almost busted my stitches." I nudged his shoulder.

"For sexting, I'm your man." He gave a crooked smile. "I was a bit worried you'd report me for sexual harassment. I could lose this sweet job. So when are you gonna start sexting me back?"

When I got home, Mom was in the backyard with Dex, smoking and painting her toenails. She'd kept her promise not to smoke in the house, which meant she was outside a lot of the time. More stress, more cigarettes. I didn't have the heart to nag her about it.

She finished painting the last toenail, then shifted her lawn chair, trying not to send smoke in my direction. "How was work?"

"Same old."

"You might as well quit that job now that you have the scholarship. Take some time off. You'll find a job on campus in the fall."

"It's all right. I have fun there sometimes. And I might need the money."

"If you're concerned about money, I'll pick up an extra shift here and there."

I knew what she was doing. Just like Ms. Halsall had wanted me to step down from the school newspaper, Mom wanted me to quit McDonald's. Ms. Halsall had been worried about stress, and I was sure that Mom was worried about safety. Although they both had the best of intentions, I couldn't go along with them.

"You work six shifts a week, Mom. And you have . . ." *A divorce to pay for*, I didn't say. "You have a mortgage. Don't worry."

She grunted. "Don't worry, huh? I hate to let you out of my sight, Maddie."

"I know. But I can't take being holed up in the house anymore." I wished I could tell her about Lobo's assurance that I was safe, but that was too big a can of worms to open. Instead I said, "Turns out the Reyes who attacked me left town. They knew the cops were after them."

"Really?" Mom asked, desperate to believe me.

"Yeah." It *might* be true. How could Lobo say I was safe if the perps hadn't left town? And if it helped Mom sleep at night, it was worth it.

Before Mom could question how I knew all of this, I changed the topic. "Don't forget, my birthday's coming up. Iz is already making plans."

"Are you going to celebrate together this year?"

"Nah, Mom, we haven't done that in years." Although our birthdays were a week apart, Iz and I had come to a decision that two parties were always better than one.

She took a drag of her cigarette and exhaled slowly. "Let's do something for your birthday, just you and me. How about the Siesta Café? You're not too cool to hang with your mom, are you?"

"Of course not. Sounds great." I knew she didn't mean anything by it, but I felt a prickle of resentment. We'd barely done any mother-daughter things in the last few years, and it wasn't because I thought she was lame company. It was because of Boyd.

I watched as Mom inspected her freshly painted toenails. "I'm off to bed, honey. Early shift tomorrow." She kissed my cheek as she got up.

"Night, Mom."

Mom went inside, and I leaned back on the lounge chair, staring up at the sky. I should probably coax Dex inside and do some work. Ortiz had sent me his quote last night, and I was eager to get going on my letter to the editor. But I was too tired to do any work right now, and it was Friday. I'd earned some chill time.

It was a clear, starry night. Watching the stars always made me think of big, overwhelming things, like the meaning of life, or the unfathomable size of the universe. Usually those questions made me uneasy, but not tonight. After all I'd been through in the past few weeks, I felt lucky, almost giddy, that I was even alive to ask those questions.

I sat up and watched Dex as he played fetch with himself. He wasn't a puppy anymore, but he still had a puppy's energy, a puppy's joy. Boyd had suppressed those things in him, but they had surfaced eventually. It felt good to see Dex enjoying himself. Ever since I'd been attacked, he'd become more aggressive. He'd even taken to sitting at the window and barking at people walking by. He wanted everybody to know that if they threatened his family, there'd be hell to pay.

"Hello," a voice said from the darkness.

My heart pounded in my chest. I surveyed the backyard, trying to pinpoint where it was coming from. The swing, I realized, not ten feet away from me. Shaded by a palm tree, a man in black was sitting on it.

"It's Lobo."

"I didn't hear you. How'd you get in here?" I'd locked the gate when I'd come in.

"I jumped the fence."

How could he have done it without Dex noticing? Dex chased down anyone who got close to the house, person *or* animal.

"Sorry I scared you," he said.

"Don't be," I said quietly, hoping Dex wouldn't hear us. "But watch out for my dog. He's gonna freak when he sees you."

"He'll be fine." Lobo snapped his fingers. "Hey, boy!"

Dex's head shot up and he ran across the yard, skidding to a halt in front of him.

"C'mere, boy." Lobo gestured with his hand for Dex to come closer, and Dex obeyed. When Lobo scruffed his neck, Dex nuzzled against him, wagging his tail happily. Then Lobo hit his rump and Dex bounded off again.

I was in shock. "How did you do that? Dex never lets any guy pet him. He hates men."

"Your dog knows a true alpha male when he sees one. He knows when to be aggressive, and when to submit. Besides, he can tell that I'm not a threat."

"He can?"

"Of course. Why'd you name him Dex, anyway?"

"I didn't. My mom's ex-husband named him after *Dexter*, that show about the serial killer. Dex used to be his dog."

"Well, he's loyal to you now."

"Yeah. But I think he's traumatized that I got hurt. Somebody walks by the house and he goes crazy. I fear for the mailman."

"He's feeding off your mom's anxiety. He'll get better once he's sure you're safe. It could take time."

"Hope you're right. Are you a dog whisperer or something?"

He chuckled softly. "I like dogs. They're honest. They never hide what they're feeling."

I bet Lobo saw the irony in his statement. He himself was hiding, crouched in the shade of the swing, cap and bandanna covering his face. If he shifted just a few inches, the moonlight might give me a chance to catch a bit of a glimpse. But he didn't budge.

"There's a war going on in Miami," he said. "I thought you should know."

His words sent a shiver through me. "What do you mean?"

"Los Reyes are fighting for territory with a Mexican cartel. The cartel's led by a kingpin called El Chueco."

I'd heard of El Chueco. His thick, pockmarked face had been all over the news lately. He planned to take over the drug trade in South Florida, and right now, the Miami gangs—especially the Reyes—were in his way. El Chueco's name meant *crooked* because of the twisted things he'd done to his enemies. Anyone who got in his way ended up brutally murdered, and their body would always turn up in a public place—that was his signature.

"Just be careful," Lobo said. "I've made sure the Reyes won't touch you. But when the cartel and the Reyes clash, anyone could be caught in the crossfire."

My stomach sank. He'd made me feel that I was safe, but it sounded like no one was safe anymore.

"Where do the Destinos fit into this?" I asked.

"We don't. Our war is different."

His tone was closed. The reporter in me was tempted to press him, but I knew he wouldn't talk. I'd better just say what I needed to say while I had the chance. "You saved my life, Lobo. Thank you. I'm sorry I didn't say that at the hospital."

"It's cool. You never needed to thank me, Madeleina."

My heart flipped over. I wanted to go to him, to open my arms to him. I didn't even care who he was. I didn't need his name or his backstory. I just wanted to be near him.

"I was hoping you'd come and see me again." The darkness made me brave, made me feel like I could say anything.

"The truth is, I've been trying not to. But I wanted to tell you about El Chueco."

I nodded. "Thanks for the warning."

He might've sighed. It was hard to tell with his bandanna. "I can't visit you again, Madeleina."

"Why not?"

"It doesn't do either of us any good. The more I see you, the harder it'll be to stay away." He grunted. "That's the irony of hiding who you are. Makes it easier to tell the truth."

"I want you to keep coming back. You don't need to tell me anything you don't want to." I heard the desperation in my voice. But I *had* to see him again. The thought of seeing him was what had kept me going since the attack.

"Why can't we, like, um . . ." My words tripped over each other. What could I say—let's hang out? Catch a movie?

"You might see me around, in the light of day. But if you did, you wouldn't know me. And I have to keep it that way."

My eyes welled up. It was crazy, but I felt like I was being dumped by the love of my life. I felt a quick spinning sensation—like I was drowning. I'd built a fantasy around Lobo, as if I could turn my masked savior into a boyfriend. A boyfriend in a bandanna.

"I'm sorry, Madeleina."

And I could tell that he was. Whatever was between us, he must've felt it too. He wouldn't be here if he didn't.

We were quiet then. Crickets came alive in the silence. I saw him get up, adjust the cap over his eyes, and move toward me. I sat as still as a statue, afraid to move.

I closed my eyes. He must've pulled down the bandanna, because I felt warm lips touch my temple. But it wasn't enough for me. It wasn't close to enough. I turned in my chair and reached up, guiding his head down to mine.

He groaned. We caught our breaths, kissing hungrily, starved for each other. My hand curled in the silky hair below his cap, and he moved back sharply, turning away and pulling up the bandanna in one quick motion.

I should probably be embarrassed that I'd grabbed him like that. But I wasn't. That kiss was all I'd have to remember him by. And I knew he'd wanted it just as much.

"Good-bye, Madeleina." He moved away.

I was alone again. And I'd never felt so lonely in my entire life.

"Good-bye, Lobo," I whispered into the darkness.

BIRTHDAY BUMPS

I WASN'T IN THE MOOD TO HAVE A BIRTHDAY this year. But as the twenty-seventh of April got closer, Iz talked about the plan nonstop. Should we go dancing? Of course. Some drinking? No doubt. A male stripper? Um, no.

I played along, but I didn't see anything worth celebrating—except maybe that I was still alive.

After Lobo's last visit, I'd fallen into a funk. The reality of everything that had happened was finally sinking in. For a while, the thought of Lobo, the mystery and excitement of him, had kept away the depression. But now that I knew he wasn't coming back, the darkness was here to stay.

I stopped seeing Jennifer, the school psychologist. She kept saying that I was depressed and needed meds. She said the meds would carry me through this time until I could deal with all that had happened to me. I couldn't explain to Jennifer that it wasn't just PTSD I was going through, it was heartbreak. Last I checked, meds couldn't fix that.

When I woke up on my birthday, I went to my Facebook page and saw a slew of messages. Ah, the love. Of course, most of those people wouldn't have any clue that it was my birthday if Facebook hadn't reminded them, but I didn't care.

My locker was decorated when I got to school. Unfortunately, it was with little sex toys that I had to tear down and hide before a dean walked by. It was sweet, though. Iz had chosen the theme Birthday Raunchiness, so I should've expected this.

I drifted through my classes, hardly paying attention, and sneaking peeks at my phone. Julia, Manny, Abby, and Carmen—they'd all sent me birthday texts. It was a boost. And I'd take what I could get.

At nine o'clock that night, I showed up at Iz's. She looked me up and down and declared "Perfecto! Absolutely perfecto!" Then she handed me a Maddie Diaz Margarita.

I was glad she approved of my look. I'd bought the black halter dress especially for tonight, pairing it up with black, high-heeled sandals with metallic studs. Birthday Sexy, if not

Birthday Raunchy. As for Iz, she rocked a tight purple top, tighter pink pants, red lipstick and a chunky blue necklace. Color-blocking all the way. A walking work of art, as usual.

"Birthday girl!" Abby hugged me. She wore a cute maxi-dress from H&M. "How was dinner with your mom?"

"Awesome. Where's Carmen?"

"Don't speak her name!" Iz hissed. "I'm ready to smack that girl stupid. She had the nerve to call and say she'd meet us at the club later. Can you believe that?"

I shrugged. "It's fine with me."

"It's not fine," Iz insisted. "Carmen's overdoin' it. I'm sick of her crashing at my place whenever she stays out late with Rafael. It's getting out of control. Even my parents are starting to get pissed off. She's doubling our water bill with her long showers."

"Carmen's parents don't even know she's dating anyone," Abby said.

"And now she blows us off on your birthday? No way. Uh-uh. It's bullshit. I'm gonna tell her when I see her."

Abby and I looked at each other. We could read each other's minds where Iz was concerned. Iz had gotten into plenty of scraps in her day. She was like a bitch-slapping Speedy Gonzales—small but fast.

"Tell her tomorrow, not tonight," Abby said. "Let's keep the peace for Maddie's birthday."

"I'll try. That's all I can say. Now it's gift time!" Iz squealed and grabbed a red gift bag.

"I told you not to . . . ," I began.

"Just open the damn thing!"

There were two sparkling silver frames with black-and-white pictures. One was of me and Iz sticking out our tongues—just hours after Iz had gotten her short-lived, soon-infected tongue piercing. The other picture was of me and Iz at the beach when we were kids, arms slung around each other.

"They're for your dorm room. I painted the frames myself."

"These are awesome." We hugged.

Iz always gave the most thoughtful gifts. I'd have to think of something good for her birthday, and I didn't have much time. It was a week from Sunday, but we'd be celebrating it next Friday.

"Now mine," Abby said, handing me a gift bag. I looked inside, and laughed when I pulled out purple lingerie.

"I've seen your underwear," Abby said. "You can't wear Hanes Her Way in college. Even your roommate will disown you."

I pulled the bra over my chest. "Verra nice."

"It's got some push-up too." She pumped her hands. "Wha' wha'. Gotta treat the girls right."

For the next couple of hours, we gossiped, listened to

music, and nodded our heads while Iz bitched about Carmen. Then we caught a cab to the club.

Nostalgica was downtown, near the Miami Dade campus. Pub by day, club by night. The doormen didn't come on until eleven, so we slipped in just in time.

Julia was waiting for us at the bar, casual beautiful in a black tank and jeans. "Happy Birthday, Maddie!" She gave me a big hug.

I noticed Iz bristle. I'd mentioned to her that Julia had visited me while I was laid up, but I hadn't said we'd become good friends. Iz had always been possessive of her friends—of me, in particular—and I knew she wouldn't like it.

"Where's Eric?" I asked Julia.

"He gets off work at midnight. Hopefully. Last week the chef kept him an hour late to drill him on how to sear a scallop."

"French chefs are hard-core," Abby said.

"The worst part is that Eric doesn't even mind staying late. He loves that shit. He's a total perfectionist in the kitchen."

"What about in the bedroom?" I asked, arching a brow.

"He's obviously fantastic—he's my cousin!" Iz said. "That kinda thing is in the blood. Now the question is, he can sear a scallop, but can he cook a clam?"

We all groaned. The Birthday Raunchiness was under way.

One drink and several dirty jokes later, we danced. The

floor was already overflowing with underage people like us who'd flooded in before the doormen came.

Julia was an awesome dancer. Her moves were natural, sensual, and Brooklyn smooth. Iz danced like a little powerhouse, arms and legs in the mix. As for Abby, she did her trademark moves—the head-groove, the "wave your hands in the air like you just don't care," and some lasso throwing. She was a tall, blond beacon, and always got surrounded by short, South American admirers.

At some point, Carmen showed up and joined our circle. Iz checked her watch and glared at her. Carmen brushed it off. She danced all sexy, putting on a show for Rafael. He'd stationed himself at the bar, watching her. It was almost creepy.

Surrounded by my good-looking friends, I didn't expect to have an admirer of my own, but I did. My eyes locked with those of a cute guy and my shy smile gave him permission to come closer. I hadn't thought I was looking for any attention, but I liked it. Soon we were smiling and dancing together. Why not?

But in the back of my mind, I kept thinking of how shallow it was to dance with some random guy when the one I really wanted was out there somewhere. Where was Lobo tonight? Was he thinking about me too?

Lobo's not coming back, I reminded myself. He'd been all too clear about that. I should move on. It was, after all, my birthday.

Then I remembered something Lobo had said—that if I ever saw him again, I wouldn't know him. What if this guy I was dancing with was Lobo?

"I'm Maddie," I said into his ear.

"CJ."

"I love this place," I said, unable to think of anything else.

"Yeah." So he wasn't a conversationalist. It didn't matter. Iz always said there was nothing worse than a talky guy. It was one of her many complaints about Rob.

But one thing was sure—this wasn't Lobo. I couldn't picture Lobo coming up to me drunk like this guy. CJ wasn't stumbling yet, but there was a vagueness in his eyes that told me he was getting there.

"Hey, happy birthday," Eric said, giving me a friendly, but not overly huggy, hug.

"You made it," I said.

"Course I made it. Iz and Julia would've gone medieval on me if I hadn't."

CJ hung back as I talked to Eric. He seemed a bit jealous, which was flattering, I guess. But when Eric went over and started dancing with Julia, CJ seemed happy to forget about the interruption.

A Rihanna ballad came on, and the dance floor dissolved into couples. Abby even accepted one of her admirers' requests for a dance. Rob hooked up with Iz, and Rafael grabbed

Carmen against him and proceeded to give her a slow, long kiss.

CJ molded his body against mine and went in for a kiss. I ducked my head away, and he ended up planting a kiss in my ear. It felt like a wet willy. I took it as a sign that I was officially done with him. Time for a strategic bathroom exit. "Sorry, CJ, but I have to go to the—"

"Happy birthday, Maddie," someone said. Despite the loud music, I knew immediately who it was.

Ortiz got between us, his eyes focused squarely on CJ. "Can I take over? Thanks, bro."

CJ's lips tightened. In a quick second, he assessed Ortiz, then made a smart decision—he backed off. "Go for it," he said, walking away.

Ortiz slid his arms around my waist as if it were the most natural thing in the world. "Once you put on the *ick* face, I thought I'd get rid of him for you."

Some small part of me melted. But another part of me was annoyed. Didn't he think I could stand up for myself?

"You didn't need to do that. I was about to cut him loose. I'm just glad he didn't take a swing at you. He was pretty drunk."

"Well, if he comes up behind me with a broken beer bottle, let me know. Anyway, that guy isn't drunk. He's on psychedelics. His whole crew is." He nudged his chin toward CJ and the two guys he'd joined at the bar. "You can't tell the difference?"

"Ah, no. Never done them myself."

"Me neither, in case you were wondering."

"I wasn't."

His eyes narrowed and he *almost* smiled.

My breath hitched. Ortiz could rattle me so easily, and he knew it. Maybe that was why he'd intervened with CJ—because he thought I was a spaz when it came to guys. And wait a minute—what was Ortiz doing here anyway?

"I meant it," he said.

"What?"

"Happy Birthday." He gave me a knowing look. "You made it this far, huh?"

"That's how I'm looking at it."

Although I hadn't drunk much tonight, I suddenly felt tipsy. I caught the scent of aftershave. Subtle, manly. He didn't have to rely on massive amounts of deodorant spray or slick clothes from the pages of *GQ* to get a girl's attention. He'd look good in a paper sack . . . or nothing at all.

Okay, so Iz was right. I *was* horny as hell.

"What are you smiling about?" he asked, a ghost of a smile on his lips.

"I was thinking of a dirty joke Iz told me. I'd tell you, but it's not for virgin ears."

His smile broadened. "I'm *all* ears now."

I loved our banter. Didn't want it to end. But the song was fading out, and the electronic beat of a fast song was rising behind it. Maybe if I could get him over to the bar, we could chat a bit more before rejoining the group.

"Can I buy you a drink?" I asked, feeling bold.

"I can't stay."

Great. Why had I even said that?

"But let me buy *you* a drink before I go," he offered.

"No, thanks. I'm pacing myself." I tried not to show what I was feeling. I couldn't believe he'd just gotten here and was blowing me off again. "Early shift in the morning?"

"Yeah, then a boxing match right after."

So he was being sensible. But I wasn't in the mood for sensible right now. Sensible sucked. This was my birthday, wasn't it?

I forced a smile. "I'm sure you'll kick ass tomorrow." Then I gave him a *thanks for coming* hug.

I knew immediately that it was a mistake—the friendly hug thing didn't work when you were attracted to someone. I felt his hands pressing into the small of my back, my breasts flattening against his chest. We held each other a little too long, then we both pulled away at the same time.

"Night, Maddie," he said, maybe with regret on his face. "See you around."

FEARLESS

"THAT WAS SO HOT WHEN ORTIZ TORE YOU AWAY from that guy," Iz said an hour later. We were at an all-night greasy spoon for our after-club eats. "I'm surprised he didn't whup the guy's ass in a jealous rage."

"I didn't see any signs of jealous rage," I said. "Ortiz is the ice-cold type."

"That's just what he lets you see," Abby pointed out. "I thought the whole thing was pretty romantic."

"He didn't want to see me with someone messed up on psychedelics," I said. "That falls under the category of civic duty. Maybe he saw the guy tongue-kiss my ear."

They both made *ew* faces.

"I hear psychedelics are the sickest trip," Iz said. "They

make you hallucinate, you know. He might've thought your ear was an ice cream cone."

Abby and I burst out laughing just as the waitress brought up our plates. We'd all gotten the restaurant's trademark dish—fries topped with gravy, bacon, and a fried egg. Total grease heaven.

After a couple of minutes of straight eating, Iz came up for air. "Next time you run into Ortiz, you're gonna end up making out with him. Gua. Ran. Teed." She fanned herself and downed some ice water. "Damn it, where's Rob when I need him?"

"You sent him home," Abby said.

"Yeah, well, he doesn't do girl talk. Not that Rafael is any better. He's never said two words to me." Iz glanced meaning-fully at the empty seat beside Abby.

"Go easy on her," I warned. "Carmen's so into him that she doesn't care what we think anymore. If you go after her too hard, she could write us off completely."

"Write us off after *how* many years of friendship? She wouldn't be that stupid." But I could tell Iz wasn't so sure.

We turned back to our food. The combo of drinking and dancing always made us ravenous.

"Oh my God." Abby's face went pale. "Do *not* look."

"What is it?" I asked, my stomach twisting.

"There's some Reyes here from Rivera. Maddie, if they see you . . ."

I spotted them immediately. One guy and three girls. I tried to remember what Abby had said about the Reyes at her school. They were part of a sub-gang called the Primas. Most of them joined because their older siblings were Reyes, a sign of solidarity.

The waitress was leading them this way.

One of the girls' eyes zeroed in on me. She put an arm out to stop the others. They all looked toward me, eyes widening. They whispered among themselves, then turned and bolted out of the restaurant.

Iz said, "Let's get the fuck out of here before they come back."

Abby was on her feet immediately. "You think they're going to get their friends?"

"I'm not risking it." Iz riffled through her purse and threw some cash on the table. "This'll cover us. Let's go." Iz gave my arm a tug. "*Andele*, baby."

I wanted to tell them there was no need to go—that I was sure the Reyes weren't coming back. But Iz and Abby hustled me out of there. We ran several blocks in our heels and didn't look back.

As I ran, a feeling of elation swept through me. I knew why the Reyes had run off, and it wasn't to get backup.

They were scared. I'd seen it on their faces.

Lobo had been right, I realized. The Reyes weren't

going to come after me.

But why were they so afraid?

"She's impossible to buy for," I told Julia the following Wednesday as we left another store.

The mall was alive with people—housewives, homies, tourists. Every store window was plastered with the promise of great sales, but I couldn't find anything that screamed Iz's name, or even whispered it. And her birthday party was two days away.

"Ah, c'mon. Everybody wants something." Julia had a chill vibe, as always. She sipped her new favorite drink, a mocha latte blanco. I'd introduced her to it.

"That's the thing. Iz has everything she wants. And if she can't afford to buy it, she freaking makes it herself with a stick, a ribbon, and a can of paint."

Julia smirked, but I was dead serious.

We scanned the stores. I should've gotten my act together sooner, of course, but I'd been distracted—more like *obsessed*—with last Friday night's surreal incident. Seeing a group of Reyes run from a possible confrontation was a first. I knew that Lobo must be behind it. But how had he managed to keep them away from me? What could he have possibly done to scare them off?

My mind spun with questions. No answers came. Just the echo of Lobo's voice reassuring me: *It doesn't matter, Madeleina. You're safe now.*

"Maddie?"

"Sorry, what?"

"What about a gift card to the craft store?"

"It's a good idea, but . . ."

"But what?"

"I just feel I should do something special, like she did for me. But I'm not crafty at all."

"I'm pretty sure she knows that by now," Julia said, obviously amused by the whole thing. "You're all riled up about this gift, aren't you?"

"I guess. I want to pay her back for wading through the shit with me, you know?"

She slanted me a look. "No gift can pay her back for that. You can only pay her back by standing by her. By being a real friend."

I cracked a smile. "You'd be great at writing greeting cards."

"True, that." Julia sighed. "Let's keep looking, then. We still have an hour till the mall closes. But I'll need another latte."

Time always flew by with Julia. There were endless things to talk about. She put a cool spin on even the most mundane topics.

My phone vibrated. A text from Iz.

Where are you?

I texted back,

Picking up your gift.

I figured it was a good choice of words, because it sounded like I was *picking up* something specific, not cruising the mall cluelessly two days before her party.

Don't bother buying me a gift. Just go wild with me
Friday night. P.S. If you've already bought it, I can't wait
to see it!

That's all I needed. More pressure.

"So you know I'm gonna bring up *your* birthday," Julia said as we were browsing an art supply store. "And you know why."

"Mr. Hot and Cold, I presume."

"Bingo."

I glanced at her, trying to gauge what she knew. "Why did he show up for all of ten minutes?"

"That's what I wanted to ask you. He met up with Eric after work. Told him he just wanted to drop in to say hi to you. It looked like you were getting pretty cozy on the dance floor."

"Not really. He just cut in to save me from a guy on psychedelics."

"The act of a modern Prince Charming." She sobered. "I hear psychedelics are the shit now. Some cartel brought them in to put the local kingpin out of business."

I expected to hear this stuff from Manny, not Julia. "You're in the know."

"I make it my business to be. There's no point in being innocent, Maddie. It's the best way to get caught in the crossfire."

"Sounds like a little Brooklyn PTSD."

She shrugged. "Not a little."

THE WHY

IN THE END, I GOT IZ A JEWELRY BOX from a Trinidadian street vendor. It wasn't your typical jewelry box—it was handpainted in bright colors and adorned with beads and feathers. The best part was that when you opened it, reggae music came out.

It was a relief, because I had a ton of newspaper stuff to finish. There was no way I'd admit that I was struggling to keep up. No way I'd show the weakness Ms. Halsall was expecting.

Thursday at lunch, I holed up in the library, choosing a study carrel in a faraway, quiet corner. I'd already spent twenty minutes going over Cassidy's article about the school's recycling program, and I was beyond bored.

Out of the corner of my eye, I noticed someone heading my way. I did a double take. "Who the hell let you in here?"

"You had me at *hell*." Manny gave a crooked grin. "So much for a secure school, huh? All I had to do was flash some prison tats and they escorted me right in, red carpet all the way."

"You're kidding me."

"Half kidding. I know Gush, one of the guards. We went to school together. He told me you were back here."

"Gush?" I'd thought I knew the names of the security guards, but I couldn't place him.

"He goes by Jenkins now, but to me he'll always be Gush. See, he used to pee his pants in grade school. Doesn't like being reminded, either."

Manny grabbed a chair from a nearby study carrel, sat down backward, and scanned the area.

"I didn't stop by just to look at your pretty face, Diaz." The usual Manny grin faded. "People are talking about you."

"That's nothing new."

"But they're saying strange things. Things that can't be true."

"Spill it, Manny."

"The rumor is that you have some connection to the cartel."

"The *what*?" I said, far too loud, then caught myself. "How could anyone think that?"

"I guess you don't know what happened to the guys who jumped you."

A wave of apprehension rolled over me. "Then fill me in."

"The three Reyes who jumped you were kidnapped and their middle fingers were cut off."

I felt like I'd been sucker punched. *"What?"*

"It's the mark of death of El Chueco's cartel," Manny said, almost apologetically. "See, once the fingers are cut, it means the next time someone in the cartel sees you, you're dead. Deal's done. So the guys who attacked you had to leave Miami fast. They had to go where they'd never risk running into a member of the cartel."

My stomach felt queasy. Lobo must be responsible for this. Had he cut the fingers off himself, or had one of his guys done it? It was so brutal. And yet, other than killing them, this must've been the only way to keep them from coming after me again.

I remembered the fear on the faces of the Reyes at the greasy spoon last Friday night. Now I knew why. They thought I was linked to the cartel.

Another thought hit me like a freight train. What if the Destinos had cut the guys' fingers off for a completely different reason?

What if they *were* the cartel?

Or at least, working with them.

It made sense. Perfect, horrible sense. The Destinos' reason for being was to screw with Salazar and the Reyes, wasn't it?

Manny studied my face, waiting for me to say something.

"This explains a lot," I said. "I ran into some Reyes last weekend and they seemed scared, like they really didn't want a confrontation."

"I wouldn't either if I thought you were linked to the cartel."

"This is unbelievable."

"I know. You don't even look Mexican."

But neither of us was laughing.

BOMBSHELL

ME AND SOME FRIENDS GOT TO SCHOOL EARLY for our birthday duties. We taped little red lipsticks to Iz's locker and wrote cute notes all over it. Then I slipped ten bucks to Candace Johnson, who did the morning announcements. Instead of the boring "Happy Birthday to Iz Moreno" crap, she promised to say, "Happy Birthday to the outrageous, outspoken, and never outdone Iz Moreno."

Iz would love that. She showed up to school dressed like a birthday bombshell, and didn't resist when we put a red feather boa around her neck. I grinned as she sashayed toward her first class.

At lunch, we sang her "Happy Birthday." Iz jumped up on the table, conducting us with the feather boa until Mr. Layton told her to get down before she fell and broke her neck.

On the bus home, Iz was pumped, because the best was yet to come. The plan was drinks at her place with the girls, then a swanky new pool hall we'd heard about. Rob would meet us there, and he'd assured us they didn't check ID.

I arrived on Iz's doorstep at eight thirty. I'd blocked off both of our birthdays ages ago. I hoped Iz liked her gift. But I could rely on her to pretend to like it even if she didn't.

Abby opened the door. "Hey, Maddie." She had an awkward look on her face, as if I'd interrupted something. "Come in."

Iz and Carmen were sprawled on the sectional, icy drinks in their hands. I was glad that Carmen was there. Iz would be pissed if she showed up late again.

"Hey, guys!" I said, but my words fell flat. They didn't seem happy to see me. I frowned. "Everything okay?"

Iz got up and walked over to me, hands on her hips.

"You were out with Julia the other night, huh?"

I frowned. "Yeah. Shopping for your gift."

"I didn't know you guys hung out so much."

"Are you being serious?" When I realized that she was, I turned to Abby for help. "I'm not sure what's going on here."

"Eric told her you've been hanging out with Julia." Her eyes said it all: proceed with caution.

I turned to Iz. "Julia and I hang out sometimes. It's not a big deal."

"I just don't get why you always hid it from me," Iz said. "It's like you thought I couldn't handle it."

It was true, and she was proving that right now. "I didn't want you to think that I was gonna ditch you for her. I'd never do that. You know that, right?"

Iz crossed her arms. "Then why didn't you ever invite me along? I always invite *you* along when I'm going out. *Always.*"

From the couch, Carmen said, "Iz was there for you when Boyd was making your life miserable. And this is how you repay her."

"Stay out of this, Carmen," Abby snapped. "This has nothing to do with you."

"Carmen's sticking up for me," Iz said, jutting out her chin. "Which is more than I can say for Maddie."

"What are you talking about?" I asked. "Since when don't I stick up for you?"

"I know Julia can't stand me. I tried to hang out with her when she first moved here, and she totally blew me off."

I felt like I was walking into a minefield. I had sensed that Julia wasn't a big fan of Iz, but I could never say that. "Julia's never said anything bad about you. It's just that we're both into writing and stuff."

"I don't care if you don't invite me along. You can hang with whoever the hell you want. But I don't appreciate you keeping things from me."

My gut sank. I wasn't doing a good job of digging myself out of this. "Look, Iz, I'm really sorry. I thought it was better to keep things, you know, separate."

Tears shimmered in her eyes. "Whatevs. I knew you were gonna ditch me sooner or later." She stalked back over to the couch to sit with Carmen, turning her back on me.

"C'mon, Iz," I said. "We can talk about this another time. Tonight's about celebrating your birthday, right?"

No response.

"Iz . . ."

"Can't you give her some space?" Carmen fired back at me. "Jeez!"

Abby gave me a helpless shrug.

That's when it hit me.

This was my cue to leave.

When I got home, I realized I was still carrying Iz's birthday gift.

Oops, I probably should have left it.

Not that she would have wanted it anyway.

Mom was out with her friend Charlene tonight. That was a relief. I didn't feel like explaining what had happened. I wasn't even sure I could explain it.

Dex followed me up to my room, where I kicked off my

shoes and put Iz's gift in my closet where I couldn't see it. I sat down on my bed.

This was the point where I was supposed to break down in tears.

But I didn't.

I'd never meant to hurt Iz. I'd only been trying to protect her from her own possessive streak. And though I was sorry it had gone down that way, I didn't feel I deserved the verbal bitch-slap I got.

I texted Abby:

Can you talk to her?

Her reply:

I'm trying. But she's really pissed off and Carmen's not helping the situation. This is so dumb. She's ruining her own birthday!

I'd pictured Iz and me being best friends forever, racing our walkers at a nursing home someday. But I wasn't sure anymore. If this was how she reacted to my friendship with Julia, how was she going to handle my new social life at college?

The doorbell rang. Dex bolted down the stairs ahead of

me. I wondered if it would be Iz and the girls in a cab, waving me in. Iz's mood could change on a dime.

But it wasn't Iz. It was Julia.

"Hey," she said. "All dressed up and nowhere to go, huh?"

"Pretty much. Come in."

We plunked down on the living room couch.

"Are you in as big trouble as Eric thinks?" she asked uneasily.

"Worse."

"Shit." Julia shook her head. "Eric feels horrible. He let it slip that you met up with us one time, and then Iz started firing all these questions at him."

I shrugged. "It's a catch-22. If I'd told her we were hanging out, she would've been pissed off. And now she's upset that I never mentioned it."

"The girl's trippin'. Eric said so himself. I know she's your best friend, but it's true."

"She's freaked out because I'm going away to college. I think that's what's behind this."

"Well, I told Eric to go without me tonight. Iz would probably hiss at me and throw holy water."

I laughed. "You should go, Julia. You've got nothing to apologize for. Be nice and show her you have nothing against her."

"Seriously?"

"Trust me. If you don't go, she'll think we're sitting here talking about her."

Julia smiled. "Which we are." She looked like she was about to get up, but then she stopped. "And Maddie, I'm sorry for all this. I never meant to come between you guys. I know what it's like to lose friends and . . . I'd never do that to you."

"I know."

I hugged her, then walked her to the door. "Now go get showered with holy water and call me tomorrow."

LIGHT OF DAY

I WOKE UP EARLY THE NEXT MORNING and checked my phone to see if I'd heard from Iz. I'd texted her twice last night offering peace and more birthday wishes.

No reply.

I double-checked my phone. Nothing.

Silence from Iz was the kiss of death. It was the last trial her boyfriends had to suffer before she dumped them. Why was she doing this? I couldn't begin to understand it.

Unable to get back to sleep, I rolled out of bed and took a shower. After throwing on a T-shirt and shorts, I went downstairs. Dex was already there, head bent into his doggie bowl. It was 6:25 a.m. and the sun wasn't fully up. Neither was Mom.

I slipped on my flip-flops, put on Dex's leash, and we headed out.

There was something about early morning walks. Since it was Saturday, the whole neighborhood was still asleep except for a handful of elderly people tending to their flower beds. The weather was blissful, warm but not yet hot, with a faint breeze. As we walked, you could see the shadows lift over the streets as the sun came up.

Dex loved an early walk too. It was the only time he owned the streets. There were few people around—especially men—to put him on edge.

We passed Sasso's, and I squinted to see if Ortiz was working. He wasn't. Good. I tied Dex and went in, pouring myself a large, dreamy-smelling hazelnut coffee. When I approached the register, I heard Dex barking. A couple of burly bikers had parked in the lot—leather clothes and leathery skin, studded up and bandannaed. I groaned and quickly paid for the coffee. Dex had probably woken up the entire neighborhood by now.

I hurried outside. The bikers were having a smoke right next to him. Couldn't they see he had personal space issues?

"Sorry," I said to them, propping my coffee on the curb and trying to untie Dex—but it was impossible with him straining at the leash.

The bikers didn't spare me a glance. Unfortunately, they were in no rush to butt out their smokes and go inside.

"Dex, calm down," I ordered sharply. "Dex, down!"

I finally got him untied and scooped up my coffee. Then Dex reared toward the bikers and snapped his teeth. Hot coffee spilled on my toes.

"Ow! Fuck, Dex!"

The bikers laughed at us and went into the store.

A black car pulled up in the lot. Ortiz's car. Crap, he must be on day shift today. I tugged Dex in the other direction, but he tugged back just as hard, barking furiously at the car. Of all the times to see Ortiz. I was a hot mess with second-degree coffee burns on my feet.

The car door opened, and Dex leaped toward it. My coffee sloshed everywhere. I tossed it in the trash, needing both my hands to stop Dex from attacking. This was so embarrassing, I couldn't bear it.

Ortiz got out of his car. "Hey, how's it going?" Not waiting for my answer, he headed for the door of Sasso's.

"Sorry, Dex goes crazy when—" I broke off, stunned. Dex was sitting on his haunches, his tail wagging cheerfully. Like a perfectly trained dog.

Thank you, Dex!

"Can't talk, I'm late for my shift," Ortiz said. "See ya later."

He went inside. I bent down and hugged Dex. "You came through, buddy! Finally learned some manners, huh?" I gave him a doggie treat.

Too bad I'd ditched my coffee. Looking over, I realized I'd overshot the garbage and it had burst all over the sidewalk. I picked up the cup and threw it out, hoping Ortiz hadn't seen me do that.

I looked down at Dex, still amazed. I'd like to think it was the beginning of a whole new Dex, but I doubted it. He had never been like that before. Ever. Except . . .

I froze in place.

Except when Lobo was around.

It had to be a coincidence. Dogs responded differently to different people. And there was something about Ortiz, a confidence that even an aggressive dog like Dex would recognize.

I glanced through the glass. Ortiz was standing at the register, a newspaper spread out on the counter. I bet he could feel me watching him, but he didn't look in my direction.

Your dog knows a true alpha male when he sees one, Lobo had said.

It hit me with shattering clarity. Dex had recognized the true alpha, but *I* hadn't. I hadn't recognized him . . . until now.

The thing about the truth is, once you know it, you can't believe you didn't see it before.

Everything fell into place.

Sasso's. *Of course.* There was nowhere in the neighborhood more central than Sasso's. It had cameras that could take in the whole block. Ortiz could eavesdrop on anybody he wanted to—gangbangers and their girls buying food, gas, smokes, or just hanging around. It was the perfect spot for him to keep tabs on the neighborhood.

I patted Dex's head. "Thanks, Dex. Thanks for helping me see."

I had to go talk to him. But I made myself wait for the bikers to leave the store. Then I tied Dex up again, gave him a handful of doggie treats, and went back in.

Ortiz glanced up from his newspaper. He looked weary, like he'd had a rough night. "Hey."

My knees trembled as I walked up to the register. I fumbled for a pack of gum, in case anyone walked in.

He rang it through. "That's one oh six."

I dug into my pocket, handing him two dollar bills. He gave me change.

I didn't move.

"You okay?" he asked.

"I know who you are. Dex gave you away."

Ortiz frowned. "I don't follow."

"Dex only reacts like that to one person. *You.*"

He glanced out the window for a long moment. Then he looked me right in the eye. "Smart dog."

His admission caught me off guard. It took me several seconds to find my words. "We need to talk," I said.

"Not here."

"Where?"

His expression was cool. "Nowhere."

I stared at him. "But . . . I *know* now."

"We'll both be safer if you forget what you know."

He was stonewalling me, damn it. I couldn't let him. Couldn't let him shut me out.

"I'm sorry," he said. "You're still better off on the outside."

"But this changes things," I insisted, flattening my hands on the counter. "It changes everything."

"No, it doesn't." For a moment, something resembling regret flickered in his eyes. His hand came over mine, squeezing it. "I trust you to keep me safe, Madeleina."

The sound of my name on his lips choked me up. "But . . ."

Behind me, the doorbell chimed. I glanced over my shoulder to see a woman with a stroller come in. When I turned back, Ortiz's expression was cool again. Blank. Like he didn't even know me. "Have a nice day," he said.

I couldn't speak. I slipped out the door, away from Lobo.

PURGATORY

IT WAS AGONY.

I hardly slept for days. Didn't think of anything but him.

I was still reeling from the fact that my late-night visitor had been Ortiz. That Ortiz was the one whose touch was gentle, but whose lips, when pressed to mine, had blown my mind.

There was no peace in knowing who Lobo really was. Ortiz was the one guy I'd been drawn to in real life, but could never get close to. And that hadn't changed.

I had so much to ask him. Why the hell was he in charge of a gang? He didn't strike me as someone who got off on violence and drama. He was tough as nails, yeah—I'd seen it in the boxing ring—but he didn't seem reckless. And the Destinos targeting the Reyes was definitely reckless. What beef did the Destinos have with them?

The questions drove me crazy. I needed to talk to him to get some answers. And then I would leave him alone, let him do what he had to do.

Except . . .

In the darkness of my bedroom, I knew that it wasn't just answers I wanted.

It was him.

Sleep-deprived and fired up by my new knowledge, I felt like a robot, going through the motions. School, homework, newspaper, rinse, repeat.

Iz didn't speak to me all week. Didn't answer my calls or texts. She made a point of slamming her locker door whenever I was around. Everyone at school knew she was mad at me, but she never told anyone why. In her mind, she might think she was taking the high road, but it was the opposite. It just made people speculate about all the terrible things I could've done to her.

It didn't help that my article on Hector had hit a standstill. I'd done all the online research I could do, and had gotten a quote from Eloise, the homeless woman Hector used to spend so much time sitting with. But it wasn't enough. The best information was on Hector's sister's Facebook page, and I didn't feel right using it without permission. But I couldn't just ask her—Detective Gutierrez had warned me early on not to have any contact with Hector's family. I was stumped on what to do.

By Friday night, all I wanted was to go home after work, crawl under a rock, and sleep. But Manny wasn't having it. "Come and play pool with me, Diaz. I know you got nothing better to do."

"Now *that*'s below the belt," I said, taking off my grease-stained apron. "You know I'm a pariah these days."

Manny smiled. "Then welcome to the dark side."

He was right; I had nothing better to do. Iz had booked Abby and Carmen days ago to go to the movies. Abby was apologetic—she hated being caught in the middle. As for Carmen, she hadn't been in touch all week. She'd obviously taken Iz's side.

I'd hung out with Julia last night, so I wasn't planning to call her tonight. I didn't want her to think I was going to be all clingy now that Iz had ditched me. According to Abby, Julia had actually approached Iz on her birthday to try to smooth things over between us. Julia had put all the blame on herself. Iz's response was to tell Julia to "stay the fuck out of it." Julia had walked away, refusing to take the bait. Julia might have the Brooklyn in her, but she was too classy to fight with Iz.

Manny drove us to a pool hall in South Beach packed with stylish people and drunk tourists. I knew why Manny had chosen to avoid the pool halls in our neighborhood—so we wouldn't run into anyone we knew. For a break from the drama.

I flubbed my first shot, hitting the edge of the white ball and sending it off in the wrong direction.

"You could go pro with shots like that," Manny said.

"Very funny."

Manny sank a corner shot and leaned on the table. "Talk to me, Diaz. Tell me what's on your mind."

"I'm sick of what's on my mind. What's on yours?"

"A hot girl whose pants I'm dying to get into."

"Manny!"

He laughed. "I didn't mean you. I meant Black Dress over there. She's my type, don't you think?"

I smirked. If his type was tall, blond, and drop-dead gorgeous, then yes, she was his type.

"Hanging out with a beauty like you is upping my value, Diaz. She just looked over. Now laugh like you're having a good time."

I laughed, and I didn't have to force it. "I *am* having a good time."

"Good. Just like that." He flashed a ridiculous, thousand-watt smile at the girl, and I laughed again.

"Okay, enough laughing. I want her to see I've got the looks to back up my sense of humor." He leaned on the table, striking a *GQ* pose, stroking his goatee. "How do my pipes look when I do this?"

"Um, good, but you're flashing your underwear."

"Oops!" He pulled up his pants. "Thanks, Diaz. You got my back."

And Manny had mine. Instead of trying to talk to me about the Iz situation, the cartel rumors, or anything else, he kept me laughing all night. Even when he struck out with the blonde, he made a joke of it.

On the way home, above the thumping car radio, I asked him how school was going.

He shrugged. "It's going all right. Got a paper due next week. I hate writing papers. Who knew you'd have to write them for heating and cooling?"

"You could ask your instructor for help. Most of them like that."

"Not this one. He judged me the first day I walked in there. Thinks I'm another dumbass ex-con who'll get locked up before I can finish the course. I'll show him."

"It sucks that he's judging you. Well, I don't know anything about heating and cooling, but I can edit your paper if you like."

"Thanks for offering, but don't worry about it." Manny stopped at a light and glanced at me. Serious Manny was showing up, if only for a moment. "When people judge me, I think of it as penance. For the shit I've done, you know?"

Actually, I didn't know. And I wasn't sure I wanted to. I liked Manny for who he was now. I'd rather not know who he was before.

"We're all works in progress, Diaz. We're all broken and bleeding and trying to fix ourselves up into something human."

"Wisdom 101 from Manny?"

"I'm not wise, but at least I'm alive. And that's more than I can say for a lot of the suckers I grew up with."

THE MESSAGE

DEX WAS MAKING IT HIS MISSION not to let me sleep in. I'd shooed him into the hallway hours ago, but he kept coming back, panting outside my door, urging me to wake up.

I stared at the ceiling. I'd been up half the night, my mind in overdrive. I'd replayed what had happened at Sasso's a hundred times. The coolness of Ortiz's expression, the regret in his eyes, the hand squeeze.

The gesture might have only been to comfort me. But I was convinced that it was more. He'd been reaching out. He'd been telling me that the Lobo who had visited me at night, the Lobo who had kissed me, was real.

"*You're still better off on the outside,*" he had said.

But he was wrong. I wasn't better off on the outside. I was

just miserable and alone.

A plan formed in my mind.

I sat up and texted Julia.

Do you think you'll see Ortiz this weekend? Can you
give him a message for me?

She replied within a couple of minutes.

He's usually at the gym Saturday aft. What should I say
to him?

Maddie: Tell him I miss him.

Julia: I love that! You're brave, girl. He obviously likes
you. This'll be the push he needs.

I didn't know if I was being brave or dumb. But I wasn't
backing down.

That afternoon, while I was cooking burgers at McDonald's,
Julia texted me back.

Mission accomplished.

My breath caught.

Maddie: How did he react?

Julia: It's hard to tell. He just nodded.

Maddie: Did he seem annoyed?

Julia: I don't think so. He only seemed annoyed when Eric told him to grow a pair and ask you out already.

Maddie: I hope I haven't pushed him too hard.

Julia: Don't worry. Ortiz will do what he wants to do. He's got a fine pair already. Not that I've peeked in the change room to find out. ☺

"We need three more Big Macs here!" Tom yelled at the front.

"On it."

Now there was nothing left to do but wait.

He would come tonight. I was sure of it. I just didn't know who would arrive—mysterious, protective Lobo or cool, closed-off

Ortiz. If I was lucky, he might answer some of my questions. If I wasn't, he'd tell me to back the fuck off.

I braced myself for either.

The moment Mom went to bed, I unlocked the gate. No sense in making Ortiz climb the fence if he didn't have to. We both knew that I was expecting him.

When I heard the faint click of the gate, my heartbeat accelerated.

He was here.

Unlike last time, he didn't stick to the shadows or retreat into the shade of the swing. He just walked in, hand in one pocket, hair ruffled by the wind. In a white T-shirt and jeans, Ortiz was the same achingly cute Corner Store Guy my friends and I had crushed on.

It hit me that *this* was Lobo, the one who had watched over me. I wanted to run into his arms, but instead I stayed put in my lounge chair. Not Dex. He ran to him, bounding up and down.

"Hey, buddy," Ortiz said, scruffing Dex's back. "You gave me away, didn't you?"

Dex's tail did a happy wag, then he returned to his bed in the grass.

"Are you angry about my message?" I asked, trying not to show how nervous I was. The porch lamp glowed behind him, making it hard to see his eyes.

"If I came here angry, don't you think Dex would've attacked?"

"I think you can make Dex believe anything you want, like you do with everyone else."

"Well, then, I'm not mad." He sat down next to me, on the same level as my chair. "But I was hoping you'd let it go."

"It's just that I have some questions."

His mouth twisted wryly. "Of course. It's the price of looking out for a newspaper editor."

"Why look out for me in the first place?"

He gazed down at his hands. Those hands had held mine, had stroked me and comforted me. I could tell that he was debating what to reveal. I held my breath and waited.

"Because you stood up for Hector. He wasn't everything he seemed, you know."

I frowned. "What do you mean?"

"He helped me out with information."

I was speechless. For two or three seconds, anyway. "He was *working* for you?"

"Yeah. Hector had an amazing memory. He could recap a whole conversation, almost word for word. It's incredible what people would say in front of him."

"My God. Is that why they killed him?"

"No. That night he was in the wrong place at the wrong time. And so were you. Not a lot of people would've spoken up for Hector. I figured it made sense to have my guys keep an eye on you."

"I tried to convince myself that the Reyes wouldn't come after me. I heard Ramon and Diego were small-time."

"It's true. They're stupid fucks whose names Salazar probably doesn't even know. He wouldn't have authorized them coming after you. It would just spell more trouble for the Reyes." I saw his hands tighten into fists, felt the tension coil in his body. There was more to Ortiz than the cute guy at the corner store. He was a gang leader. He exuded power.

"I'm surprised you didn't just tell me I was in danger. I would've let the cops know."

He glanced at me, eyes narrowed. "This isn't the first grade. Officer Friendly doesn't come to anybody's rescue. I'm sure you know that by now. The cops aren't your friends."

"But the Destinos are?"

He shrugged one shoulder. "Seems that way, doesn't it?"

I straightened. "No more talking in questions. No more vague answers. I want to understand the Destinos—what their purpose is."

"You don't stop, do you?" He dropped his eyes. "Maybe that's why I can't get you out of my head."

The admission melted me. If he thought of me half as much as I thought of him, then he must be going crazy too. I was tempted to reach for him. But I cautioned myself to stay in check, to keep my distance.

Ortiz met my gaze. "If you really want to know about us, I'll show you. But the truth is ugly."

"I don't care."

"Then will you come with me, Madeleina?" He reached out his hand.

A strange feeling came over me. If I took his hand, my life would change forever.

I grasped it. "I'm in."

DARKNESS

WE DIDN'T TALK IN THE CAR. He was in his thoughts, and I was in mine.

Wherever he was taking me, it was north of the city. He drove along the coast, the ocean a streak of blackness against the horizon.

The moonroof was open and the scent of the night was all around us, the rush of air in our ears. I saw a sign saying, "Fort Lauderdale, The Venice of America," and I wondered why a city would want to associate itself with Venice when everybody knew that it was sinking.

All I knew about Fort Lauderdale was that old people and spring breakers flocked there like geese. It wasn't a place you'd expect someone like Ortiz to know well, but he navigated the streets easily, making plenty of twists and turns. I wondered if he was deliberately making things confusing so I wouldn't remember where the place was.

"In case we're being followed," he explained.

"You think someone is tailing us?"

"No. It's just protocol."

He pulled into the driveway of a ranch-style bungalow in a middle-class neighborhood. He parked in the back, got out of the car, and came around to open my door before I'd even gotten my seat belt off. As we walked toward the house, he took my hand. His touch sent a shiver up and down my arm, even though I knew he wasn't being romantic. It was to guide me.

He led me in the back door. The house was cheerful inside, but dated, with yellow wallpaper and flowery curtains, old-fashioned furniture, and knickknacks everywhere. The walls held pictures of a family over several generations—white, mostly blond, with big teeth.

Off the kitchen were a couple of steps leading to a basement door. Ortiz did a rhythmic knock.

Seconds later, the door opened.

Standing there was a built, blue-eyed guy dressed entirely in black. A flash of memory came to me. He was the one who'd carried me from the scene.

The guy seemed just as startled to see me. "You brought her?"

"I did," Ortiz said in a *don't even bother* tone.

The guy's jaw flexed, but he didn't argue. He stepped aside.

Down a flight of stairs was a basement apartment. It had several connecting rooms off the main living area. A blonde with long, tanned legs was watching a small TV. She turned our way, scrutinizing me like I was a weird bug. "Who's that?"

"Maddie," Ortiz said.

"Ah." Smug smile. "Witness girl, huh?"

"Yeah," Ortiz said. "How's Taylor?"

"Sick. Very sick."

"How much longer?"

She shrugged. "Two days. Maybe three."

"We have a day and a half, that's it. Methadone?"

"We're almost out."

"Shit," he said, raking a hand through his hair. "We'll get more. Gimme a day."

I knew what methadone was. It was a drug used to help people detox from other, harder drugs.

"Come with me." Ortiz led me down a hall and knocked on the first door.

"Yeah," croaked a female voice on the other side.

My grip tightened on Ortiz's hand. This was the ugly he'd been talking about. *This*, what we were about to see.

He opened the door, and I was hit by the smell of sickness.

The ugly, it turned out, was a pretty girl. Or had been once. She was too thin. Sallow skin, limp hair, dead eyes.

"This is my friend, Madeleina," Ortiz said. He spoke gently, like a doctor. "How bad today, Taylor?"

"Ten."

"Yesterday was a ten. How about a nine?"

"Yesterday was a fucking eleven."

"Don't worry," he said. I knew that warm, comforting voice—it was Lobo's voice. "Tomorrow will be better."

She snorted, and lit a cigarette. "I wanna go for a walk."

"Not now. But you can go watch a movie with Kelsey."

"Are you deaf? I said I need a walk. Some fresh air."

It seemed like a reasonable request, considering the size and stink of this room. But Ortiz shook his head. "Not yet. I'm sorry."

"Not yet. Right." I could feel the cold fury in her. She pulled the cigarette out of her mouth and for a second, I thought she might throw it at him. Instead, she said, "Get the fuck out of here."

We left the room. Ortiz closed the door behind us.

In the low-ceilinged, cramped hallway, we stood against each other. His eyes were inches above mine.

"Can't you let her go for a walk? She seems so miserable."

"No. She might run. We can't risk it." He searched my eyes. "We're trying to save her life."

"I can see that. So this is what you do—you bring drug addicts here to detox. To get clean."

"The drugs are only part of the picture. They're a tool the Reyes use to control the girls. So they can make money off them." He watched me carefully. "Do you see?"

I did. And it was worse, so much worse, than I'd thought.

"This is what the Destinos do, Madeleina. Salazar traffics these girls. We try to find them, get them out."

I nodded, holding back tears.

Ortiz's eyes were hard, glittering. "You wanted to know why, Madeleina. This is why. This is why Salazar has to go down."

Ortiz didn't take me home after that. He wanted to eat, so we stopped at a diner. My stomach was one big knot, but I ordered food so he wouldn't have to eat alone.

"What will happen to Taylor?" I asked quietly.

"She's lucky. Her brother's coming for her from California. She's from a good home."

"But most aren't—from a good home, I mean." I knew it from the research I'd done last year. Most of the girls who got caught in sex trafficking were runaways. It was incredible to think that they'd left troubled homes only to become prey to traffickers.

"Some girls are from the projects—others from behind a white picket fence," Ortiz said. "What they've got in common is, they're all running from something."

"And they end up in a far worse situation than they started out in."

He nodded. "Then there are the other girls, the foreign ones. Brought here with false promises of jobs. Salazar has recruiters in several countries and he posts ads on the internet. This is big business for him—bigger than the drugs or the gun-running."

"What happens to those girls, the foreign ones, after you rescue them?"

He sighed. "Some of the embassies help. Others are so corrupt we won't even drop them off there. We try to get in touch with their families. Try to find any way possible to get them home."

Something occurred to me. "Those girls in the newspaper. From Honduras. Were you behind that?"

He nodded grimly. "We couldn't find a way to get them out, and one of the girls was very sick. So we tipped off the cops as a last resort. They're at the Honduran embassy now. I hear they're talking. That's good. Some girls are too afraid to talk."

We went quiet as the waitress refilled his coffee. When she left, he looked up at me. "I hope I didn't make a mistake showing you this."

"You didn't."

"I wanted you to understand." He looked away for a second, as if wondering whether he should say more. "I lied to you, Madeleina, when I said I was hoping you'd let it go. I wanted to let you in."

Reaching across the table, I put my hand over his.

"I want to help. Any way I can."

"You don't have to do anything. But maybe *this*." He glanced down at our hands. "Maybe . . . you and me."

THE BEACH

I TWIRLED SPAGHETTI AROUND MY FORK IN A DAZE. The same daze I'd been in all day. I was reeling from the euphoria of being with Ortiz, and the horror he had shown me.

Mom watched me eat. Stared, actually. She had no clue that I'd been out all night, and was obviously wondering why I'd called in sick to work and had lain around in my pajamas all day.

"Have you and Iz made up yet?" she finally asked. So that's why she thought I'd been sluggish today. She thought I was depressed about Iz. Made sense.

"Iz is just being Iz. It'll blow over. She did the same thing to me in seventh grade. It lasted a week."

"I remember. It's definitely seventh-grade behavior. All

this because you were spending time with Julia?"

I nodded. "Abby keeps trying to talk her down, but she's not done punishing me yet."

"I'm sorry you're going through this, Maddie. Iz hasn't changed for as long as we've known her. Still as melodramatic as ever. On the upside, she's a lot of fun. The downside's the temper."

"True, and true."

She gave me a pointed look. "Don't forget, there's nothing she wouldn't do for you."

"Except *talk* to me," I said with an eye roll. "But yeah, I know what you mean."

"I wonder if she's jealous of all the attention you've been getting lately."

"Jealous? She wouldn't want to be in my shoes, Mom. No one would."

"Not consciously. But you see this sort of thing in the siblings of drug addicts. They can be resentful of all the attention the addict is getting."

"It's not a bad theory." I raised my brows. "Dr. Drew?"

"You got me." She smiled. "Don't you worry, honey. Iz will come back. And when she does, don't give her too hard a time, okay? She's flawed but . . . we all are."

"I know, Mom."

At that moment, my phone lit up.

It was Ortiz. I'd had a feeling it would be.

Last night when he'd dropped me off, there'd been no "I'll call you" or "See you later." We both knew we'd be together as soon as possible.

Ortiz: Dinner time?

I smiled. I'd forgotten how much he knew about me—my work schedule, my routines.

Maddie: Tasty spaghetti. Join us?

Ortiz: No thanks. But I'd like to see you tonight. You game?

Maddie: Yes.

Ortiz: I can be there at 8.

Maddie: See you then.

I put down the phone, feeling a rush of adrenaline. An hour and fourteen minutes until I'd see him again.

"Sorry," I said. Mom hated when I texted at the table. Usually I didn't.

"Who was that?"

"It's . . . this guy I'm seeing tonight."

Mom's mouth dropped open. "You have a date?" Shock quickly became panic. "You should've checked with me. Who is he?"

"Ortiz." I didn't know his first name, but I wasn't going to admit that. "He's a good friend of Eric's."

She put a hand to her chest, relieved. A friend of a friend was always a good thing. "How old is he?"

I didn't know that either. "Maybe twenty. You actually know him already. He's the cute guy who works at Sasso's."

She tilted her head. I could tell she was mentally scanning her interactions with him. Then she relaxed some more. "He's always been nice, polite."

"We're just hanging out," I assured her. "Don't worry, Mom. I trust Ortiz. And . . . he's looking out for me."

At eight o'clock, the doorbell rang. Dex skidded to the door, and Mom grabbed his leash.

"It's all right, Mom. You can let him go."

She gave me a *yeah, right* look and kept hold of the leash.

I opened the door. The second Dex saw Ortiz, he sat down, wagging his tail. Ortiz got down on one knee and petted Dex.

In shock, Mom mouthed to me, "Are you serious?"

"Dex loves him," I mouthed back.

Ortiz got up and said, "Nice to see you, Mrs. Diaz."

Ortiz was all confidence. He had the *you can trust your daughter with me* role down to a tee.

"Nice to see you, too," Mom said. "Where are you headed tonight?"

He turned to me. "A walk on the beach, maybe? Then a coffee?"

"Sounds great," I said, grabbing a sweater.

Mom nodded with approval. As we stepped out the door, she said, "Have fun, but not too much."

I rolled my eyes.

The dark cabin of the car was thick with electricity as he pulled out of the driveway. "You look really good," he said, glancing my way.

"Thanks." I'd put more than the usual effort in, but hopefully he couldn't tell. I wore my favorite jeans, the faded ones that time had molded to my body, and a white lace shirt with a black cami underneath. I'd initially undone three buttons, which would give him a good peek of cleavage, but the moment I'd heard the doorbell, I'd chickened out and done up two of them.

"I like when you come into the store early in the morning in that big T-shirt and flip-flops," Ortiz said.

I laughed. "Yeah, right."

"I'm serious," he said with a huskiness that made me shiver.

"So are we really going to the beach?" I asked.

"Yeah. We can talk there without any worries."

We reached the beach in minutes, and Ortiz parked at a strip mall lined with cheesy tourist shops.

The boardwalk was pretty at night. Colorful lights from the hotels and casinos reflected off the water. There was a coolness in the air, so I put on my sweater.

Ortiz took my hand and we walked for a while. Whatever this was, this connection between us, it didn't need words.

"I wanted to bring you here because this is where it started. The Destinos, I mean. It's where we made a pact to take down Salazar."

"How many of you are there?" I asked.

"Twelve."

"Seriously? From your reputation, I'd have thought there were more."

"Good. That's what we want people to think. Believe it or not, twelve of us can do a lot of damage."

"You guys have proven that. How did you find each other?"

"On the streets. Some of them met in juvie. We were all magnets that stuck together, whether we wanted to or not."

"Destiny," I said.

"Yeah. I told them what I planned to do. Told them the risks. I had a mission, and I think they all needed one."

I watched him, waiting for an answer to the big, obvious question—why was he doing this?

Ortiz reached into his coat pocket and handed me a neatly folded piece of paper. I opened it.

> Dear Daniel,
>
> My dream was an illusion. But please don't let your dreams die. I hope that in death I can watch over you better than I have in life. I'm so sorry to leave you.
>
> Love always, Andrea

My hand trembled. "Are you Daniel?"

"Yes. It's from my sister."

"What does it mean?"

He gazed out at the water. It took him a while to find his voice. "I'm from Houston, Madeleina. The shit-hole side of Houston. My mom was . . . I think she was bipolar, but she was such a heavy user it was hard to tell. She died when I was ten and Andrea was fourteen. Auntie did the best she could for us, but she already had three kids." His mouth twitched, and I could see that it was hard for him to get the words out. "My sister had big dreams for me. She thought I'd go to college, be a big shot someday. She saw an ad online about nanny positions in Miami. Figured she'd moved down here for a couple years and save up some cash. So we could have a better life, the two of us." He looked out at the horizon. "That was the illusion."

My heart was in my throat.

"There was no job. They locked her in an apartment, shot her up with drugs, and sent in one john after another. She fought. I know she fought. But she had no chance."

Tears filled my eyes. "Oh, God."

"She did it for me. That's the thing. Her dream was for me." For a few moments, he was far away. I felt the rage pulse through him, the grief. When he came back, his voice was perfectly calm. "She escaped, eventually. I don't even know how she pulled it off on her own, with all the security Salazar puts on the girls, but she did. It was too late, though. She was so broken that she only wanted to escape so she could end it. And she sent me this letter."

I started to cry, and reached out to touch his arm. "I'm so sorry."

"Yeah. Me too."

There was a hollowness in his voice that scared me. Like he'd been hurt so much he'd gone cold.

"She wouldn't want you to feel responsible," I said.

"I know. It's ironic, though. This letter was supposed to

bring me peace. To tell me to move on." He shook his head. "I couldn't do that. Not when I knew there were others like her."

"I can't speak for her, but I'm not sure that she'd want you to risk your life for this. I bet she'd want you to be safe."

"If not me, then who will help those girls?" He looked at me, as if I could actually answer him. "Who?"

But I had no answer.

"It's satisfying, you know. It really is. When I help a girl, I feel better. Every time I fuck with Salazar, I'm happier."

I knew there'd be no talking him out of this. No coaxing him to a safer path. Ortiz was determined to shut Salazar down no matter what the cost.

Even if it was his own life.

SMOKE AND FIRE

AFTER THE BEACH, ORTIZ BROUGHT ME TO A BAR in Little Havana filled with cigar smoke and grizzled Cuban men. But I didn't for a second think he'd taken me to the wrong place. The music was the real thing—pure, soulful salsa played by a lone man in a red fedora.

Ortiz led me to an isolated table in a dark corner of the bar. We sat with our backs to a brick wall, pressed close together.

"The performers are always good," he said. "I come here sometimes to relax."

I wasn't feeling relaxed right now. Maybe I should try to kiss him. Would that cut the tension between us, or amp it up?

He was studying my face. My lips, to be exact. I suspected we were thinking the same thing. Suddenly shy, I looked away and tried to focus on the guy playing music. I tapped my foot, and he put a hand down on my knee. I wasn't sure if he wanted to feel more of me, or if he was trying to steady me.

"Don't be nervous," he said. I wished, for once, that he wasn't so good at reading people. I wanted to project confidence, not jitters.

I turned to him. His face was inches from mine, and so beautiful. "Do you, um, come here with the guys?"

"No. We don't go out together. Too risky. I come here alone."

"Oh." I fought for something else to say. "So how do you know so much about dogs, anyway?"

"My neighborhood was full of *perros callejeros*—street dogs. Someone had to keep them in line."

"You're a born leader. Of dogs. Of people."

He shrugged. "Aren't you in charge of your school newspaper?"

"Yeah, but it's not so easy for me. I'm no alpha dog."

"Are you sure about that? You're different from most people. You've got a leader's strong energy, but you can play the beta role, too. Like with that friend of yours. The one who was always hitting on me at Sasso's."

"Iz. We're not exactly friends anymore."

He looked surprised. "Why not?"

"Because I've been hanging out with Julia and she feels left out. She called it a betrayal."

"Strong words. You gonna patch things up with her?"

"Hopefully. If she decides to talk to me again."

The compassion in his eyes surprised me. After all he'd gone through, he actually felt bad about my broken friendship with Iz?

"She doesn't know who she is without you. But you know who you are without her. That's the problem."

"How can you tell?" I doubted he was watching Dr. Drew like my mom.

He shrugged. "It's just what I see."

"You see a lot."

"Hope that doesn't creep you out."

"Only a little." Then I smiled. "Your instincts have kept me safe." That brought something to mind. I might as well go for it. "I need to ask you a question—about the Reyes who attacked me."

I felt him draw back slightly. I'd gone and killed the mood. But I just couldn't let this go.

"You said it yourself, Madeleina. I've kept you safe."

"I know but . . . people are saying I'm connected to the cartel. You know why, right?"

"Yes," he said firmly. "There was no other way."

I turned away from him. I couldn't stand to think of Ortiz or one of his guys cutting off people's fingers, no matter who they were or what they'd planned to do to me.

Ortiz brought my face back to his. "It was that or kill them. If we'd killed them, we'd have even more Reyes to deal with. And I've never killed anyone. The *only* thing that would scare off the Reyes is the cartel."

"You're not working with the cartel, are you?"

"Of course not. Never. Is that what you thought?"

"I didn't know what to think."

His mouth made a grim line. "The cartel deals in drugs, not girls. But they're just as sick as the Reyes, trust me." His hand reached out to touch my face. "I'd do anything to protect you, Madeleina. Anything."

"Why?"

His hand fell away. He looked at me as if to say, *You really don't know?*

"You're the one who works with words, Madeleina. Not me. Anything I say's gonna sound phony, like a line from a soap opera." His eyes burned into mine, as if he could make me understand. "The strangest thing happened to me that night at Eric's party. It's like you've been with me ever since. In my head, I talk to you, and you get me. In my head, I think about you and what I want to say to you and . . . do to you."

I swallowed, overwhelmed. And then his mouth was on mine. It was more than a kiss. I breathed him in and our mouths slanted, kissing deeper, devouring each other. My hands fisted the back of his jacket, pulling him closer. I felt him groan, and then his body ground against mine, pressing me into the brick wall.

He muttered something against my ear, something in Spanish, and I felt his lips and teeth against my neck, then he was back to my lips, his tongue sliding in my mouth. I was on a roller coaster, hanging on to him, desperate for him.

My mind flashed with images—of his body against mine, of what it would be like to be naked against him—of me grabbing and tearing at him and urging him on.

We both pulled back at the same time, breathless. Before things got completely out of control.

"Holy fuck." His hazel eyes had gone quicksilver. His mouth was half open, still hungry, as if he were debating pulling me to him again.

I was gripping his jacket, both holding him close and keeping him away. The kiss in my backyard had been restrained need. This one had been raw, feral hunger.

We'd both known the hunger was there—we'd touched the edge of the fire before. But it still left us stunned.

He took me home at midnight. We had a brief kiss in the dark of the car, then pressed our foreheads together.

"I want you with me," he said roughly. "All the time. Day and night."

"Me too. Are you heading home?"

"No." He sat back, gathering himself. "We're moving someone tonight. Two hours from now."

"Will you text me when you get home? Just so I know you're safe?"

Something in his eyes softened. "I will."

THE RIGHT REASONS

CAFÉ VARADERO WAS MY FAVORITE PEOPLE-WATCHING place on Calle Ocho. It was modeled off an old country Cuban home, with worn, antique furniture, vintage lamps, and faded family photos. Miami hipsters came here for overpriced snacks and fancy versions of Cuban coffees. Naturally I had to show Julia the place.

She walked into the café in blue high-tops, white jeans, and a tight black tee—part street, part chic, part laissez-faire.

"Well, fuck me," she said when she saw my smile. "You are *so* far gone, Maddie Diaz. When did you see Ortiz?"

"Saturday night. Sunday night." I slid her drink across the table. "Bought you a cortadito. No mocha latte blancos here."

She took a sip. "Mmm. What's in it?"

"Espresso with milk."

"Nice, I'll get yours next time. So. Your message must've woken him up, huh?"

"I think so. Thanks for your help."

Julia grinned. "Thank *you*. I'm sure he'll go easier on Eric in the ring if he can release some of that pent-up sexual energy. Get ready, girl. He's a raging bull."

"Giddy up." I had more than enough pent-up sexual energy of my own.

We both laughed, and I felt a pang, realizing it was the sort of raunchy girl talk I usually had with Iz.

Julia must've read my face, because she said, "Eric told me Iz and Rob broke up yesterday."

I lifted a shoulder. "The poor guy's days were numbered. I'm surprised she didn't cut him loose sooner."

"That's the weird thing. Rob dumped *her*."

"Really? Rob was so into her."

"Eric said she was totally blindsided. She was bawling on the phone."

"Bawling?" That didn't sound like Iz at all. I figured I'd text her later to ask if she was okay. She would probably ignore it, but it was worth a shot.

Julia sat back and sipped her drink, taking in the café and its young, stylish crowd. "Sweet place. I should bring my laptop here some time. We could have a study date."

"Think we'd get anything done?"

"Probably not." She smiled. "What were you working on, anyway?"

"The tribute to Hector."

"Did Ortiz ever send you a quote?"

"Yeah. It's perfect." I opened my laptop and read it to her. "'Hector was a gentleman. He always had a smile on his face and a kind word for everyone. The most grateful, humble person I've met.'"

"Didn't know Ortiz was so eloquent."

"Me neither. I got another powerful quote from Hector's friend Eloise. 'Shared everything he had, even if he had next to nothing.'" I sighed. "I have a few more quotes, and I've written up a biography but . . . there's something missing. I need a *personal* account of his past and his family life. His sister wrote some great stuff on her Facebook page, but I can't exactly email her to ask permission. I'm not allowed to have any contact with Hector's family before the trial."

"As far as I know, you don't need permission to quote her page. I'd have to double-check, but I think it's all public."

"It might be, but it still wouldn't feel right."

"How about I email her for you? I'll tell her I'm a college student who thinks Hector deserves better treatment in the press. Then I'll ask if she's okay with her Facebook page being quoted. I can say it all without actually lying. Up to you."

I thought about it. I wanted my letter to the editor to be as punchy as possible, and I just couldn't do it without using the information from his sister. It was worth a shot, anyway.

"Okay, let's do it."

Julia snapped her fingers. "Consider it done."

True to her word, Julia got it done.

At nine thirty that night, she texted me:

Vicky Rodriguez Sanchez says you can use anything on her page, pics and all. She said, "I'm so glad you're doing this."

I replied:

Thanks, Julia, you're the best.

It was the green light I'd needed. I went straight to her Facebook page. It was all there. Hector's life story. Hector as a kind big brother. Hector's battle with mental illness. Hector's drinking problem and homelessness. I pulled several quotes and made notes on key events in his life. The Rodriguez family had been loving and supportive, a unit that had stayed strong despite Hector's illness. I couldn't help but think of what Ortiz had told me about his own mother.

Every family has something, I wrote. *A crisis, a tragedy, a struggle. Hector's family was no different.*

Once I'd made some notes, I dove in. Like automatic writing guided by a spirit, I just kept going.

The following night, I stood in the hallway outside Ortiz's apartment. I took a breath, ready to see Lobo's lair.

Ortiz twisted his key in the lock and opened the door. It was a large studio apartment. Not stylish, but neat and clean. The usual furniture was there—a futon that acted as both bed and couch, a TV, a couple of tables and lamps. The only thing that surprised me was the books. Two stuffed, mismatched bookshelves lined one wall.

"Keeping it simple," he said, neither proud nor embarrassed.

I searched for something to compliment, but there weren't many options. "It's a nice size for a studio."

He smirked. This was one of the shadiest areas of Miami. Not exactly prime real estate.

I spotted a piece of art on the wall, the only thing resembling decoration. It was an urban streetscape done entirely in black chalk. I approached it. The style was familiar. I noticed the X signature at the bottom.

"Eric has something like this at his place," I said.

"I introduced him to the artist's work."

"He signs all his paintings with an X? Doesn't he want to use his name?"

"That *is* his name." I sensed that Ortiz knew more, but he wasn't giving anything away.

I shrugged and went to the window, gazing down at the street corner. I spotted three prostitutes waiting for johns. We were in the heart of the city's sex trade.

"I can keep an eye on things from here."

Letting the curtain fall back, I turned to him. "You're on duty twenty-four/seven, aren't you?"

"Yeah." He shoved his hands in his pockets. "Want a drink?"

"Sure. What've you got?"

He opened the fridge, which was stocked with several types of soda and energy drinks. "Hey, I work at Sasso's. I get them half price."

"Those energy drinks aren't good for you."

"I don't have more than one a day."

"I'll have a Coke, please."

He passed me a can. "Wait. I should be giving it to you in a glass, shouldn't I?"

I smiled. "This is fine."

"Sorry. I haven't had a girl over since I moved here."

"When was that?"

"A year and a half ago."

"Really?"

"Really." He didn't need to explain, but he seemed to want to. "There's no point in having a relationship if you can't let someone in. And I've never trusted anyone but my Destinos until now."

I raised my eyebrows. He must know that a guy with his looks didn't need to have a *relationship*. He could have whatever he wanted, whenever he wanted it. That was his power.

"I don't use girls, Madeleina."

I nodded. But a part of me wondered if he could really be this perfect. My eyes narrowed just a little. "C'mon, not even the party girls? The ones who offer themselves up with no strings?"

"I'm not a saint. I won't say I haven't made mistakes. But those party girls, they're the neediest of all. They use sex to kill the loneliness."

"But it doesn't work."

"No, it doesn't."

"So how do *you* kill the loneliness?"

"The Destinos are my family. We're a pack. We rely on each other to survive."

I sipped my Coke. "I get why you want to help those girls. What about the other guys?"

"Each one has his own reason. They know this isn't a game, that it's their lives on the line. They've all been in some kind of trouble in the past. Gangs, crime, whatever. They only know this way of life. That may be hard for you to understand. But at least, now, they're doing it for the right reasons."

Silence fell between us. I walked up to the bookshelf, browsing the titles. Turned out he was a fan of thrillers.

"When do you have time to read?"

"Helps me fall asleep."

"Thrillers help you sleep?" I glanced at him, taking in the lean, hard physique, the five o'clock shadow and unruly dark hair. Desire slithered through me.

As I turned back to the bookshelf, I felt him come up behind me. He must have sensed it, my need for him. He reached past me to pick a graphic novel off the shelf.

"First book of the Walking Dead. Brilliant."

He was standing so close, I could feel his chest rise and fall against my back. And if I didn't just imagine it, he was breathing harder than he had been a minute ago.

Ortiz's left arm came up under mine, lightly brushing against my breast as he grabbed another book. "Anything by Lee Child."

"I've never read him. But if I need a bedtime story . . . "

"I'll read it to you."

His hands came down on my shoulders. Then I felt his lips on my neck.

"Here's the thing, Madeleina," he said against my skin. "When I said you're all over my mind, I meant it." He molded his body to mine. "You're all through me, all the time."

He twisted me around, and then we were kissing. The force of his need made me tremble—set my whole body on fire. This wasn't some perfectly choreographed Hollywood kiss. This was us, starved for each other.

His lips were on the exposed skin of my shoulder. "I can hardly sleep, you know. I've been dying to kiss you again, to feel your skin. So soft." He slid down the straps of my cami. I was so out of breath that I realized I was thrusting up my chest, giving him an eyeful. "God, you're killing me."

My breath rose on a laugh. It was ridiculous that gorgeous Ortiz wanted *me*, Maddie Diaz. But right now I felt beautiful and sexy—sexy enough to be his match.

The futon bumped against our legs. We must have moved toward it. All I knew was we were sinking down. I pulled his shirt over his head and whipped it away. Holy shit. I'd seen his chest in the boxing ring, but now, up close, I could feel its tightness under my hands, trace every chisel of muscle and bone. My hands went lower, and his abs rippled under my hands. I saw that he was straining against his jeans, and I cupped him over the denim.

He sucked in a breath, muttering curses in Spanish.

Then we were lying on the futon together. My cami was at my waist now, and I was suddenly glad I'd worn the silky purple bra Abby had given me for my birthday. We grappled for each other, so eager we were almost rough, and soon I was in nothing but my bra and panties, and he in black boxer briefs. I tensed up a bit, wondering at what point I should say something, let him know that I was up for this and more but not all the way, not yet. But I didn't need to say a word, because he whispered, "Don't worry. Just this."

Ortiz knew me so well, knew exactly what assurance I needed. I relaxed, giving myself up to the bliss. And he kissed me so thoroughly I lost the need to breathe.

GUNSHOT

ANYONE WATCHING US WOULD SAY WE were either drunk or in love.

Later that night, we drove to South Miami to go to Ortiz's favorite pizza place. We were both super hungry, and ordered their specialty, the Everything But the Kitchen Sink pizza. As we sat in a booth, chowed down, and chatted about all sorts of things, I couldn't stop smiling. Neither could he.

There was no break in the conversation, no need to think of what to say next. We talked like old friends who knew each other well, or new friends who were fascinated with each other. One of us could start a thought and the other would either finish it or turn it upside down. That's how we rolled.

"So what's the goal?" he asked me. "You want to write for

the *New York Times* or anchor the CBS Evening News?"

From most people, the question might be a joke, but not from Ortiz. He seemed to believe I could do whatever I wanted.

"I like the idea of investigative journalism for big newspapers or newsmagazines. Or even doing mini documentaries for *60 Minutes* or some show like that."

He nodded. "I could see you doing either. You'd be great."

I waved my hand, as if to say "stop it," but I was grateful for his vote of confidence. "So what's your goal? If, you know . . . " *If Salazar was shut down and you were free to do something else.* There was no need to finish the thought. "One of the helping professions, maybe? Doctor, firefighter, social worker?"

For some reason, that last one made him laugh. "Social worker? No, that's not me. Not really."

"What, then? You'd be an amazing dog trainer."

He smiled, knowing I was part kidding, part not kidding. "I'd be a cop."

"Yeah, right. You think most cops are corrupt."

"Exactly."

It was official: there was nothing about Ortiz that didn't amaze me.

"We need good cops," he said. "Ones that won't take bribes, or walk away from a situation because they don't want the paperwork. At the boxing gym, a lot of guys want to be cops. They want the uniform and the gun so they can strut around looking tough. Not me. And I don't plan to stay a beat cop either. I want to work my way up to lieutenant so I can have a real impact."

"Sounds like a plan to me." There wasn't a doubt in my mind that he could get where he wanted to be.

If he ever moved on from the Destinos.

We were both thinking the same thing, but it seemed an unwritten rule that we weren't going to talk about the Destinos anymore tonight. Tonight was just about us.

We stayed another few minutes, then got back into his car. He took the highway north, blasting hip hop on the radio. The dashboard clock said eleven thirty, so I'd be back just in time for my midnight curfew.

His phone rang. "Yeah," he answered. His body tightened up behind the steering wheel. "Shit. I'll meet you at the parking lot."

He put down the phone, driving a lot faster now. "We've got an emergency. I don't have time to take you home. I'll have to drop you off somewhere. I'll give you money for a cab." He changed lanes, heading for the turnoff.

"What's happening?"

"Two girls in Wynwood. We got a tip that they're about to be moved, so we have to get them out now. If we lose them, we might not find them again."

"Wait! Don't turn off. Keep going."

"I'm not taking you with me."

I couldn't let him do this. "You want to risk the girls' lives so you can drop me off? You don't have time."

He was in the turnoff lane now, but I could feel his hesitation. "Forget it. I don't want you—"

"I'll stay out of the way, I promise. For God's sake, don't turn off."

"Damn it." At the last minute, he veered out of the turn lane. "Promise me you'll do what I tell you."

"Fine."

He pressed harder on the gas.

"Why do you think they're moving the girls?" I asked.

"Salazar is upping his security, moving girls more often. Trying to throw us off."

"So what are you going to do?"

"What we always do. Bust some doors down."

Ten minutes later, he exited the highway, made a few sharp turns, and drove into a shopping mall parking lot. A gray car was parked at the north end under a tree. Ortiz pulled up next to it.

The doors of the car opened and four guys got out. They were dressed in black, bandannas around their necks. The guys looked pumped up, like football players before a championship game. When I got out of the car, their eyes widened in surprise.

"No time to bring her home," Ortiz said. "How close are the others, X?" he asked the driver of the car.

I recognized him. He was the blue-eyed guy who had helped me the night of my attack, the one I'd also seen at the safe house.

"Ten minutes, maybe fifteen," X replied. "There's no time, Lobo. I've been watching the place. They could be moving them right now."

Ortiz nodded. "Me and Rubio will take the goons." He indicated a huge guy, easily six-foot-four and two-fifty, whose fists glittered with brass knuckles.

Ortiz turned to the other two guys. One was short but built like a tank; the other was taller and leaner, with a scar slashing down one side of his face. "Felix, Matador, you get the girls out."

Then Ortiz looked at the driver again. "X, do your thing."

X smiled. "Sure, Lobo."

"Let's do this, Destinos." Ortiz smacked a fist into his palm, and the group split up. Three of them got back into X's car. Rubio got into the passenger seat of Ortiz's car, and I slid into the back.

Ortiz gave me instructions as he drove. "When we get out of the car, sit in the driver's seat. If anyone approaches who isn't one of us, drive away. You drive, right?"

"Yeah," I said.

"The plan is to put the girls in X's car so he can drive them to the safe house. But we always have a backup plan. Tonight it's you."

I swallowed. "What do you mean?"

"If the Reyes arrive on the scene, X will become the decoy, and we'll put the girls in this car instead. So if you see X drive off, put the engine on and wait. Got it?"

"Got it." My mind was spinning. This was way too intense.

"One last thing," Ortiz said. "*Don't* wait for me. If the girls end up in this car, the priority is to get them to the safe house. One of the guys will drive." Ortiz flashed a look back at me. "We're almost there. You ready?"

"Yes." Though I was far from it.

Ortiz pulled up to the curb. "We're out." He cut the engine and the lights. Then he and Rubio got out of the car and slipped out of sight, engulfed by the darkness.

I climbed into the driver's seat, staying low. The clock on the dash read 12:02.

About four car-lengths in front of me, X was in his car. The other two Destinos must have gotten out already. His motor was running, but he'd shut off his lights.

My heart pounded in my ears. One second, one heartbeat. Another second, another heartbeat. I was trying to remember everything Ortiz had said to me. *If someone approaches the car, leave. If X drives off, turn on the engine and wait.*

Gunshots rang out. I almost jumped out of my skin. Shouting erupted from the nearby projects.

I gripped the wheel, telling myself to stay calm.

A minute passed. Maybe two. A car sped around the corner.

I ducked. Oh my God. More of Salazar's guys must be here. How the hell had they gotten here so fast?

Tires squealed. I glanced up through the steering wheel, and saw X's car speed off so fast that it could break the sound barrier. The other car chased after it.

I turned the engine on. Suddenly the back door opened and three people piled in. Two girls and one of the Destinos.

"Go!" the Destino shouted, pulling down his bandanna and gasping for breath. "Drive!"

I glanced back. It was the scarred Destino called Matador. He was cradling his arm, his face contorted in pain. The two girls were huddled together, silent and bewildered.

Drive? I had no idea where I was going. And what about Ortiz and the rest of the guys?

"I said, *go!*" he repeated.

I put the car into drive and pressed on the gas, blasting us forward.

"Head to the parkway."

I tried to remember which way the parkway was. When I hesitated at a stop sign, he said, "Left, then straight for a while."

"Okay." *I can do this*, I told myself. It's what Ortiz asked me to do.

"Do you need to go to a hospital?"

"I'll be fine," he said through gritted teeth. "We need to get the girls to the safe house, then I'll get sewed up."

Glancing in the rearview mirror, I saw one of the girls wrapping a blanket around his arm and applying pressure. They knew that he had helped them, and they wanted to help him.

If Matador had been shot, what about Ortiz? I'd heard multiple gunshots.

"Is Lobo okay?" I asked.

"He and the others are handling the goons. There were more of them than we thought."

Handling the goons. Like it was still happening.

"Can't we pick him up? I could circle back. What if he's hurt too?"

"No, you can't. That isn't the plan."

Matador was right. Ortiz knew what he was doing, and I had to trust him. My hands tightened around the wheel, but I kept going.

PENANCE

I PULLED INTO THE DRIVEWAY OF THE SAFE HOUSE, parking around back. Kelsey was standing at the back door. She swung it open, waving us in. The girls needed no urging.

"Matador is still in the car," I said to Kelsey. "He needs to go to a hospital."

Her eyes widened. Then she snatched the keys from my hand. "I'll take him to get help. Look after the girls until I get back." She hurried past me.

The girls were standing in the hallway, very close to each other. For the first time, I got a good look at them. They might be eighteen and twenty, short, South American. They looked so much alike, they could be sisters.

"This way." I led them downstairs, locking the basement

door behind us.

I didn't know what Kelsey expected me to do, but I figured the basics—food, hygiene, somewhere to sleep. "*Tienen hambre?*" I asked, hoping there was food in the kitchen.

"*Sí,*" the girls said.

"Okay." I pointed down the hall to the bathroom. *"El cuarto de baño, la ducha?"* I showed them a corner closet stocked with clothes and fresh linens that I'd spotted on my last visit.

The girls nodded gratefully and went into the bathroom together. I heard the water running.

The fridge was decently stocked. I quickly scrambled eggs and buttered toast and brought the tray back to the main room. By then, the girls had emerged from the bathroom and were watching TV. They were now wearing clean, oversized sweats.

"Huevos?" I said, and they eagerly accepted the plates, thanking me.

I was tempted to sit down for a minute, but it was better to keep busy. If I stopped to think, I might start to panic. Ortiz still wasn't back. No one was.

He's going to be fine. He knows how to handle himself.

I checked out the bedrooms. They both had clean linens, some books and magazines. I wondered where Taylor was now and how she was doing. I'd probably never know.

The smell of vomit still hung in her room, but I couldn't

crack the window, since it had been nailed shut. I went to the kitchen and found some herbal tea in the cupboard—it had Russian lettering on it, but also a picture of a lemon—so I dropped two bags into a pot and heated up the water in the microwave. I brought the steeping tea into the bedroom.

I dared a look at my phone. 1:31 a.m. Where was Ortiz? Shouldn't he be back by now? But then, he and the other two guys didn't have a car. They would've had to find a safe location, then call other Destinos for a ride. That could take a while.

I saw a text from my mom. She'd sent me several while I was driving, demanding to know where I was and why I was missing curfew.

I texted back:

> So sorry Mom. We ended up at a party out of town and fell asleep. Don't worry, we're not drinking. I'll be home as soon as possible. Go to bed. Love ya.

I hoped it was enough to calm Mom down. There was nothing else I could do.

I heard a rhythmic knock at the basement door and ran up the stairs. "It's Kelsey," she called.

Damn it. I'd hoped it was Ortiz.

I opened the door. "How's Matador?"

"Fine. One of our Destinos is sewing him up."

I frowned. "Are you serious?"

"He knows what he's doing. Look, the Reyes know they shot him. They're probably searching the hospitals to see if someone got admitted with a gunshot wound. We're lucky; the bullet grazed him. He'll be fine."

I followed her back down the stairs. The girls were laughing at a TV show, their empty plates stacked on the coffee table.

"First the high of freedom, then the low of detox," Kelsey said.

"How long before it hits them?"

"By morning they'll be needing a fix."

We watched the girls in silence. I was about to ask her what else I could do to help when she said, "They were me six months ago. Lobo must've told you."

I shook my head. "He hasn't told me about anyone's past."

"So he didn't tell you I was Salazar's girl?"

I was stunned. "No, he didn't tell me that."

Her smile was cynical. "That's our Lobo. Makes the rules and follows them too."

There was a sharp knock at the basement door, and Kelsey went upstairs to open it. My heart rose in my throat, hoping Ortiz would appear. But it was X, the driver, who came down the stairs.

"Are they back?" he asked Kelsey.

"Not yet," she said.

X's blue eyes settled on me. He was an intimidating guy, as tall as Ortiz, with broad shoulders and a nose that might've once been broken. "Good job tonight, Maddie." He strode past me toward the kitchen.

His name was familiar, and now it hit me why. I wondered if he was the artist who'd drawn the pictures on Eric's and Ortiz's walls. But that wasn't my main concern right now. I hurried after him. "You haven't heard from Lobo?"

"Don't worry. No one-eight-sevens came up." He poured a glass of water.

"No what?"

Kelsey came up behind me, not-so-subtly placing herself between me and X. "He means that no homicides came in on the police scanner."

"If somebody'd got shot or needed an ambulance, I'd know about it." A faint smile came to his mouth. "I took the Reyes on one helluva ride. Lured them to a bog and made them wreck their car. They're probably still stuck in there."

"Hells yeah." Kelsey pumped her fist like a cheerleader. "Nice work, X. Too bad you didn't torch their car with that flame thrower of yours. Watch the motherfuckers burn."

X grunted and downed his water. He didn't seem to share her bloodlust. But then, why would he? It was Kelsey who must've experienced the cruelty of the Reyes firsthand, not him.

Kelsey slid past X to pour herself some water, and I noticed the way her body sidled up against him. X's face was expressionless, but I guessed that he wasn't on the same page.

"I'm going back out to see if I can find the guys," he told us. "Call if you need me." He headed for the stairs. Kelsey watched him walk away.

"Hot damn," she said, hands on her hips. It was admiration and lust and frustration all in one.

"Have you told him you're into him?"

She snorted. "He said *no thanks*. Said it's because of Lobo's rule that none of the Destinos can get with the girls."

It sounded like a good rule to me. The last thing the girls needed was to be preyed on by the Destinos. But from what I could tell, Kelsey was practically a Destino herself now.

"He's probably using the rule as an excuse," she said. "I'm damaged goods to him. Like *he* should judge. He's the one who spent years locked up."

"I don't know much about X, but I doubt he'd judge you based on . . . something that wasn't your fault."

"Don't be so sure. I wasn't some innocent girl picked up off the streets. Or some European chick snatched from a stripper pole into a bedroom. Salazar was my boyfriend."

"Oh." That took a second to process. I could see that she

was watching my face for a sign of judgment. I didn't give it to her. "I'm sure you didn't know who Salazar was when you started dating him."

"True. I met him at a club when I was a freshman at U. of M. His handlers said he wanted to meet me. I felt like a model who'd been scouted." She laughed without humor. "He's not even good-looking. But he's like a president or a celebrity. Felt like a privilege just to get near him. Is that fucked up or what?"

It *was* fucked up. "Power's seductive. Lots of people get pulled in before they know what they're in for. How'd you find out what he was really into?"

"I figured out pretty quick that he was a big-time gang leader. Not the rest, though. Not the sex trafficking." She eyed me. "I bet you're thinking—what a cliché. Suburban girl who wants to roll with a bad boy."

"I wasn't thinking that. I was thinking it's good that you got away from him when you did."

"Didn't exactly work that way. He threw *me* out like a piece of trash. I wasn't hooked on anything then. Well, except for the power."

The power—of being Salazar's girl.

"I could've gotten out, free and clear. Should've gone back to Mommy and Daddy in Boca Raton, gotten my shit together, and gone back to school. But no. I didn't want to let go of him. So I started hanging with his entourage. I wanted to stay close in case Salazar wanted me back. And sometimes, he did. For a night, anyway." She glanced at me, suddenly self-conscious. "*He* was my addiction."

"Sometimes people get in so deep they can't see straight."

She smirked. "You're right about not seeing straight. I used psychedelics with his guys. We were fucked up half the time."

"You got out, that's what matters. Kudos to you for staying and helping out the Destinos."

"Yeah, well. I owe them. It's our resident hard-ass Lobo who got me out, just when I was ready to end it."

I swallowed. I couldn't imagine how low she must've been to consider taking her own life—and I was amazed that she could talk about it so casually. "He must've heard you needed help."

"Trust me, I was *beyond* help. But here I am." She did a little bounce, again reminding me of a cheerleader. "You'd never know, would you?"

"You'd never know." Some people's pasts were easy to guess. The piercings and chains of street kids, the tattoos of gang members like Manny. But anyone seeing Kelsey would see a pretty, stylish blonde with the world at her feet.

Except for her eyes. That's where the darkness lived. She might've gotten away from Salazar, but she wasn't healed yet.

"Have you thought of going home?"

She heaved a sigh. "I *could*. But Boca Raton is boring as

hell. At least here, I'm useful." She turned to me. "This little operation we've got going—it can't last, you know."

"What do you mean?"

"Salazar's going to deal with the cartel. And once he does, the Destinos are gonna be his top priority. I've told Lobo we should go dark for a while. But he won't shut down if he has any leads to work with. It's not in him to stop."

She was right. To Ortiz, every girl was his sister. How could he walk away?

"Do the Destinos feel the same way as you?" I asked.

"They won't talk about it. As long as Lobo is in, they're in. Hell, I'm in too. Maybe *you* can talk some sense into him. Otherwise, this is a suicide mission."

A knock at the door jarred us. Kelsey hurried upstairs, unlocking the basement door. I saw Ortiz and the other three Destinos standing there. Relief swept through me.

Ortiz came downstairs, blood-stained and exhausted. He hugged me.

"Thank God," I said.

"Sorry it took so long." He held me tight. "Sorry for everything."

"You have nothing to be sorry for."

"Yeah, I do," he said against my hair. "Now let's get you home."

MAKEUP

I CREPT IN THE DOOR AT THREE THIRTY, hoping not to wake Mom. But then I saw movement on the couch, and she flicked a light on. "*Finally*," she said.

"I'm sorry, Mom. We went to this party and—"

She waved away the explanations. "I'm too tired to hear it now. I'm going to bed." She shuffled toward the stairs. "Oh, and you're grounded for a week."

"Okay."

She did a double take, then shrugged and went up to bed.

All things considered, it could've been worse.

Mom had her revenge at seven that morning when she knocked on my door. "Don't even think about missing school."

I rolled over, pulling the pillow over my face. It took all

my willpower to drag myself out of bed and into the shower.

On the bus, I gazed out the window. So many mind-blowing things had happened last night, but I was fixated on the last moments of the night—Ortiz's good-night kiss. He'd cupped my face in his hands, apologized to me for the night's events, and kissed me softly.

Last night had been surreal in every way. Ortiz had let me far deeper into his world than he'd ever intended to. And yet his world, somehow, felt more real than the world I lived in.

When I got to school, I hurried to my locker, determined to grab a cafeteria coffee before first period. I'd probably need several to get me through the day, since I had to be awake for the newspaper meeting at noon.

"So I hear you've snatched up Corner Store Guy."

I looked up in surprise. Since when was Iz speaking to me?

"You heard right."

"I'm proud of you."

A sarcastic reply came to mind, but I didn't think she was trying to be snarky. In fact, her eyes looked puffy, as if she might've been crying.

"Thanks," I said, and turned to walk away.

"Guess you're over it now, huh?" she said, stopping me in my tracks.

I knew what "it" meant: our friendship.

I shrugged. "Hey, I made my case a million times. And

you made your decision."

"Who said I made a decision? I just needed time to cool down."

Now *that* was overdoing it. "Time to cool down? I'm not one of your lackey boyfriends, Iz. I don't play those games. You know that."

Iz paled. Belatedly, I realized I'd hit a nerve.

"The lackey dumped me. Thanks for the text. I guess Julia told you, huh?"

I nodded. No point in denying it.

"It was a bad scene, Maddie. You know how he was always telling me he loved me, but I never said it back? Well, suddenly he up and says that he deserves better. Can you believe it?"

"I'm sorry, Iz." Normally this would be when I'd hug her, but not anymore. "Sounds like it was for the best. I mean, you didn't love him, did you?"

"Not yet, but I think I was getting there." Her eyes misted up. "He said I didn't appreciate him."

I'd rarely seen Iz this emotional, especially in the middle of the school hallway. I didn't know what to say.

"He was right. I was a bitch to him. And to you." Her eyes dropped. "Honestly, I don't know why I'm like that."

As far as Iz was concerned, that was an apology.

"We're cool, Iz." I couldn't promise things were going to

be the same—I didn't know. But I wanted the dark cloud over us gone already.

She managed a smile. "I could make Maddie Diaz Margaritas tomorrow night."

"Can't. I'm grounded."

"You're kidding me. You're never grounded. What did you do?"

"I was out late with Ortiz."

"You bad girl!" Iz's face lit up. "Tell me *everything.*"

I stepped away from the grill to check my face in my compact. A little shiny, but nothing a few dabs of powder couldn't fix. Ortiz was going to stop by tonight if he could get someone to cover for him at Sasso's. We hadn't seen each other since early yesterday morning, and that was too long.

"What is this, America's Next Top Model?" Manny said through his microphone. "Two Junior Chickens up here."

I quickly put away the compact. "Got it."

Manny turned and said through the shelves of burgers, "Don't worry, Diaz, you look great. I'm sure your G-Zone is flawless."

"I think you mean T-Zone."

He winked. "That too."

I laughed and kept working. Every few minutes I moved

away from the grill and glanced toward the door to see if Ortiz had arrived. Since Tom was flexible on when we took our breaks, I'd wait until he came to take mine. *If* he could get away from the store.

I'd almost given up hope when I spotted him. He didn't know I'd seen him yet, and I kind of liked that. I loved watching the way he moved, his eyes narrowing as he looked around and then warming when he finally saw me.

"Can I take my break now?" I called to Tom.

"Go for it."

Taking off my apron, I left the kitchen and went to the staff room with Ortiz. It was empty, thankfully.

"I missed you," I said, wrapping my arms around him.

"Me, too." He kissed me slowly, thoroughly. When he finally pulled back, he glanced over at Ronald McDonald. "That thing is creepy."

"I know. It's like he's watching us."

We settled in chairs facing away from the statue.

"I feel shitty that I got you in trouble," he said. "I want to speak to your mom, tell her it was my fault."

"You don't have to. But I'll tell her you offered—she'll like that."

I wanted to talk to him about Kelsey's concerns, and ask him how the rescued girls were doing. But we couldn't risk discussing Destinos business here.

"Did you read before bed last night?" I asked.

He shook his head. "I was too distracted. By you."

I smiled, and we kissed again. If we couldn't talk openly, at least we could do this . . . as long as we kept it under control.

The door swung open, and we hastily broke apart. Manny took in the scene, gave an awkward, "Oops!" then left again.

Crap. I hadn't meant to rub my new relationship in his face. But Manny *had* mentioned a few girls lately, so maybe it wasn't a big deal.

"He's not happy," Ortiz said. The Lobo part of him never missed a thing. He could read people just as well as he could read animals.

"Manny's a good friend."

"He wants to be more." Ortiz didn't sound jealous, just matter-of-fact.

"Yeah, well. It makes things awkward sometimes."

"I'll bet."

"I want to know how we're going to see each other again," I said, changing the subject. "I'm not going to wait until next Thursday. Any ideas?"

His eyes glittered. "One."

Hours later, I sat in the backyard watching Dex do what he did best—dig holes in the lawn. I should probably have stopped him, but the backyard was such a mess with Boyd's junk that I didn't bother. Besides, he deserved his fun.

And so did I. Glancing down at my phone, I saw that it was almost midnight.

When I heard the telltale click of the gate, I knew he was there. I stood up, and Ortiz's strong arms encircled me. Dex jumped up against us, wanting to be part of the hug. Ortiz bent down and played with him, giving Dex an attention fix before sending him off to dig holes again.

"I can't stay for long." He took a step back, his arms falling away.

Disappointment deflated me. I wanted us to spend hours out here, curled up together under the stars.

"Tell me what you know about Manny Soto."

"Manny?" He was the last person I expected him to bring up. "He's just a friend from work. Why?"

"Your friend is a former Reyes."

His words sank into me like a stone. I knew that Manny had been in a gang before he went to prison. But he'd never said which one, and I hadn't asked.

"Who your friends are is your business," Ortiz said, shoving his hands in his pockets. "But with those tattoos . . . I wanted to know his story, so I put some Destinos on it. Turns out Manny used to run the streets with the Reyes a few years ago. Then he got put away. Did he tell you what he got sent to prison for?"

I shook my head. "I don't want to know. He's turned his life around."

"You seem pretty sure about that."

"I am." But I had a nervous feeling inside, like Ortiz was going to tell me anyway. "Whatever Manny did, that's in his past. He's a good person."

"A lot of people think Manny didn't do what he went in for," he said. "But he confessed to the crime anyway."

"You think the Reyes forced him to confess?"

"Either that, or he cut a deal with them."

I didn't understand. "What kind of deal?"

"Maybe he wanted out of the gang, and taking the fall for someone else was his way to do it. He spent a year in juvie, then two in adult prison. That's a short sentence for his crime."

I steeled myself. "Okay, tell me. What was it?"

"Manslaughter. There was a bar fight. Manny and a bunch of Reyes were there. A guy's head got kicked in and he died."

I felt sick to my stomach. "Manny didn't kill him." I knew it for sure. He would never do something like that. "Poor Manny. Locked up for three years for something he didn't do."

Ortiz gave a grunt. "Trust me, Manny Soto was no choir-boy. And the Reyes would've protected him in prison. That's more than you can say for most guys. When he got out, he could walk away from the gang, start a new life. I've never heard of anybody getting a second chance like that. You think it's a tragedy? I'd call it a fairy tale."

He was right. Manny *was* one of the lucky ones.

We were quiet for a while. Eventually he said, "You were really helpful to us the other night. But I promise you'll never be in a situation like that again. I don't want you involved."

"I told you, I was happy to help. And I have to admit, it was . . . exhilarating." I hesitated, but realized this was my chance to bring it up. "I had a talk with Kelsey while you were gone. She's worried about the Destinos. She doesn't think you guys can keep doing this much longer."

"I know. She has a one-way bus ticket home but she refuses to use it."

"No one agrees with her that it's getting too dangerous?"

"It was *always* dangerous. Always will be. We have to change our methods constantly to stay ahead of Salazar. But we're not done. Nowhere near it."

"So you're going to keep on until . . ."

"Until we shut down his operation."

"And how would you do that?"

"We have to kill Salazar, or have him locked up. He runs the whole business himself, has a finger on every button. Doesn't trust anyone. But he's been underground for months, mostly because of the cartel. El Chueco's got a price on his head."

"Hopefully El Chueco will take care of him for you." I

couldn't believe we were talking about killing someone. Then again, it was someone responsible for destroying so many lives.

"We can't stand by waiting for El Chueco to get rid of him for us. Too many girls need our help now."

If Kelsey had hoped I'd talk him down, I was doing a miserable job of it. The problem was that I didn't know what I wanted him to do. I mean, I wanted him to be safe. But I also wanted him to help the girls.

All I could say was the truth. "I want to be with you. Even if I can't help at all . . . just promise me you'll never shut me out."

"I promise." He opened his hand, revealing a small note. "It's information. In case something happens to me. Hopefully you'll never have to open it."

Before I could protest, he put up a hand. "I'm not being morbid, all right? Just take this. Keep it somewhere very, very safe."

"What is it?"

"Details of a safety deposit box. And X's phone number. If you ever need help, go to him."

"Why X?"

"If shit goes down, he's the most likely to stay alive."

My stomach clenched. "You're scaring me."

"Come on, Madeleina. You're not easily scared. Not anymore. This is reality. If something happens to me, do something good with the money. Give it to a place that—" he broke off, thinking about it, "that helps people start over."

"What about *you* starting over?"

"That's what I'm hoping for, once Salazar is done. I want a new life. With you."

"I want that too," I said, slipping into his embrace. *More than you can imagine.*

KNOWING

THE NEXT MORNING, I CAME DOWN TO EGGS Benny and tomato salad. Mom hugged me and we sat down to eat. Even though I was grounded, she was being really nice. Maybe because, unlike in the Boyd days, I wasn't giving attitude. That must've thrown her off.

After a few bites, Mom cleared her throat. "I talked to Carrington yesterday. He says the divorce should be final next week."

My fork clattered against my plate. "Boyd's going to sign the papers?"

"He's run out of excuses not to. I doubt he'll risk another fine for skipping court. The judge won't put up with it."

"Better not. It's almost over, Mom. Can you believe it?"

"It's been a long time. Almost as long as the years he lived here." She gave me an apologetic look I knew well. Although she'd never said the words, I could feel how sorry she was.

I took a bite of eggs. "So good."

"We could have Ortiz over for brunch sometime."

"Really?"

She nodded.

"He wants to apologize to you personally for Wednesday night. But I told him he didn't need to."

"He wants to talk to me?" Mom nodded approvingly. "That's mature of him."

I smiled. "He's the best, Mom. You'll see."

At noon, I arrived at McDonald's for my shift. Manny gave me his trademark crooked smile. It didn't exactly put me at ease, but it helped. I reminded myself that he wasn't aware I knew his secret. All he knew was that he'd caught me making out with a guy.

Deep down, I'd known that Manny could have been involved with the Reyes. He had always seemed to know so much about their operation. And he'd said himself that he had plenty of things to atone for. But the Manny I knew was a good person.

"Break time?" I asked him around three, when the lunch rush ended.

He nodded. "Me, too."

In the staff room, he sat down with a Big Mac combo, while I grabbed a protein bar and water bottle from my knapsack. The guy was like a garbage disposal—he could shove it all in there, but you could never tell where it went on his lanky frame.

"Hope you're not pissed at me, Diaz," he said after a long sip of his drink. "I felt like an asshat walking in on you guys like that."

That was one thing about Manny—he never beat around the bush.

I felt my cheeks heat up. "Forget about it."

"So he's your boyfriend, huh?" He put a fist to his chest. "My heart's bleeding. Bleeding like . . . a pig?"

"You ooze poetry." But it was a relief that he was making light of it.

"So who's Mr. Right Now, anyway?"

"Ortiz. He works at Sasso's."

"I knew I'd seen that kid around. He treats you good?"

"Yeah, why? Will you put a cap in his ass if he doesn't?"

He laughed. "Nah, I don't roll like that. I'd do like my Irish grandma's people do. I'd smash his kneecaps so he's gimping around."

I tried to smile, but I had to wonder if Manny had hurt people in the past. It was hard to believe that he could inflict anything but annoyance or amusement.

Manny watched me closely. "Don't go all awkward on me now, Diaz. We're friends, right?"

"Right."

"Good." He shoveled in some fries. "I'm cool with that until you come to your senses."

The following week, I put the final touches on my letter to the editor. I polished it until it was as close to perfection as I could make it, and then sent it to the *Miami Herald*.

It was the last week of May. I was as busy as ever, finishing my last term paper and getting ready for exams. The grad issue of the newspaper was almost done, and Ms. Halsall said it was the best she'd seen in years. In other words, she was sorry she'd doubted me.

But no amount of work could stop me from worrying about Ortiz. I hardly slept, and when I did, I had nightmares. It was always some version of the same—he was hurt and I couldn't get to him. Or lost, and I couldn't find him.

One night I woke at three a.m., gripped by panic. *Where was Ortiz right now? Was he okay?* I grabbed my phone to text him, but then I stopped myself; he wasn't working a graveyard shift tonight at Sasso's, so my text would probably wake him.

I lay back down, taking a slow, deep breath, wishing I could shake Kelsey's words from my head: *This is a suicide mission.*

Even if she was right, there was nothing I could do about it. I couldn't talk Ortiz out of being a Destino. He knew the risks. He wouldn't have given me that note if he wasn't aware of how dangerous his situation was.

The note. It was tucked inside my mattress cover at the foot of my bed. He'd said to look at it only in case something happened to him. But what if there was information in there I needed to know and I couldn't get home fast enough?

I slipped out of bed and fumbled under the mattress cover. Ortiz might not want me doing this, but he didn't have to know. At the very least, I could put X's number into my phone under a fake name. That wouldn't put him at risk, and seemed like a smart precaution.

I opened the note, and nearly choked when I read the first line.

Dear Madeleina,

If you're reading this, I'm probably dead.

I don't regret forming the Destinos or the things we've done. I only regret leaving you.

X's number is 555-2813. He doesn't have a fixed address. If he has to go dark quickly, he could be hard to find. Take the scroll of artwork from my wall and show it to some

street kids in Miami Gardens. Someone will
know how to contact him.

There is a safety deposit box in my
name at Bank of America. Account number
0632004222. I've put you and X on the
account. There's at least a hundred grand in
there, blood money from the Reyes. Please
give it to charity.

If I haven't told you yet, then I'll say it
now, just so you never doubt it. I love you
and always will.

Ortiz

I stared at the note, frozen in time.

He loved me.

Friday night, Iz invited the girls over to celebrate that I was no longer grounded. Like old times, Iz handed me a drink the second I stepped in the door. It was big, blue, and icy.

"What's this?" I took a sip, bracing for it to be strong. It was.

"I'm calling them Frothy Freedoms in honor of your escape from maternal tyranny."

"Yum." I handed her the birthday gift. "This is for you." I

hadn't wanted to present it at school. "Better late than never, huh?"

Iz looked at me apologetically, then nodded. "Damn right." She immediately unwrapped the jewelry box, and snapped a picture of us holding it.

Carmen swung her bare legs off the sectional so I could sit down. We said an awkward hello. Since Iz and I were cool now, Carmen and I were too, supposedly. We both knew she'd taken Iz's side, but it was better left alone. Carmen and I hadn't connected for a while now anyway.

"So tell me about Corner Store Guy," Carmen said. "I'm dying for the deets."

"You should post pics of you guys," Iz said. "You make a gorgeous couple."

"What does he do besides work at Sasso's?" Carmen asked. "Does he go to school?"

"Nope, but he wants to be a cop someday."

"Every guy has a cop phase," Carmen said dismissively. "It's hard to get into, you know. They want more than a high school diploma."

"Who the fuck cares what he does?" Iz said. "He could be a *GQ* model, for God's sake."

Thankfully, Abby took the talk in another direction: celebrity gossip. Then we turned on *Fashion Police* and judged the good, bad, and ugly of the latest styles.

It was surreal, sitting around with the girls. So familiar, and yet so different. I'd made the decision to forgive Iz, but I wouldn't ever forget how she'd turned on me. I'd always have to be careful with her, and be prepared for whatever drama she might throw my way.

As for Carmen, I just didn't know anymore.

Rafael planned to pick her up around eleven. She told Iz that she'd be back later to sleep over, and Iz didn't protest. I had the feeling that Iz's conflict with me had made her put aside her annoyance with Carmen.

"Could Rafael drop me off too?" Abby wanted to know.

Carmen shrugged. "I'll ask him."

I was staying over tonight. Iz really wanted me to, and even though I preferred my own bed, I'd agreed.

Carmen hovered by the window. The second Rafael arrived, she and Abby went out to the car.

"Rafael never comes to the door," Iz said once they'd left. "He's too lazy."

"Is he that bad?"

"I don't know. We've hardly spoken."

We watched more TV and ate some delicious, if sloppy, leftovers from her mom and stepdad's food truck.

"Hope I'm not keeping you from Ortiz," Iz said, sounding insecure.

"Of course not. He's working tonight anyway."

"Hey. I've been wanting to ask you. Did you ever see Lobo again?"

The burrito caught in my throat, and I calmly took a sip of my drink. I'd almost forgotten that I'd told her about Lobo while I was in the hospital.

"Nah. And I don't think Ortiz would appreciate another guy on the scene."

"What if Ortiz *is* Lobo?"

Something inside me stilled, but I shoved in some food. "Huh?" I said, garbling the word. "Where'd that come from?"

"Think about it. You said that Lobo had this sexiness about him, right? And then Ortiz asks you out right after the attack."

"Lobo had a totally different vibe from Ortiz. Plus he was shorter and stockier. There's no way." I took another drink. "Kudos for trying."

She sighed and sank back into the easy chair. "Damn. I thought that would be so cool, you know. The Destinos are such badasses. I heard last week that they burst into the house of some Reyes and robbed them blind. Left the Reyes a bloody mess. Bet you love hearing that, huh?"

"Sure do." She must be talking about last Wednesday night. The Reyes would have leaked those details so that the neighborhood would feel the Destinos had gone too far. Of course, there was no mention of the *real* reason the Destinos had busted into that house.

I glanced at Iz, a sinking feeling inside me. Had she told anyone about Lobo helping me? Or that she'd suspected Ortiz could be Lobo?

Of course not. Iz knew that to even imply that Ortiz was Lobo would put him in danger. And she wouldn't be that stupid. At least, I hoped not.

THE PROMISE

SATURDAY NIGHT I TOOK A CAB TO ORTIZ'S PLACE, where he met me on the sidewalk. His arms went around me and my heart filled up.

I remembered something Mom had once told me—that there was a difference between being *in* love with someone and loving someone. Being in love was that wild, exhilarating feeling of needing to be with them every moment. Loving someone was a pledge to care about them forever. To make their happiness as important as your own.

I was in love with Ortiz. *And* I loved him.

Wordlessly, we went up to his apartment. He double-locked the door behind us and we sat down on the futon, glued to each other.

"I'm always worried about you. It's tearing me up." His

note haunted me, but I couldn't tell him I'd read it.

He brushed a lock of hair from my eyes. "I wish I could take that away from you."

It wasn't the answer I'd hoped for. I wanted him to tell me that he was going to be fine. But he was too damned honest to give me false promises. He knew what he was up against. The note had said it all.

"I keep thinking of what Kelsey said. That the Destinos can't last. That you're not safe."

"Stop thinking about it, then."

"I wish it were that easy. I have a lot of things *not* to think about. What should I think about, then?"

He took my face in his hands. "This." And he kissed me.

Kissed me senseless. Kissed me like he would never, ever stop.

This is the drug, I thought. The drug I'd happily OD on for the rest of my life. The drug I'd do anything for. Who needed psychedelics when this feeling existed?

After a while, we forced ourselves apart. He got us bottles of water from the fridge, and I was tempted to splash the cold water over both of us, but I knew a water fight would only result in more making out.

"I read your latest article," he said, leaning back into the futon. "The one about what to expect at college. It was really good."

"You read it?"

"Sure. I've read most of your stuff."

That was a surprise. I knew *Prep Talk* was archived on the school's website, but I couldn't believe he'd actually read my articles.

"You have some cool things ahead in the fall. That's what you should be thinking about."

"Next year was a lot more appealing before I met you. Will you come and see me?"

He took a drink of his water. "I'll try."

Something inside me crumbled. *I'll try* wasn't a promise. It wasn't anything.

"It's hard for me to get away," he said. "But in a few months, things could be different. Salazar could be out of the picture."

That gave me some hope. "You think so?"

"I'm gonna do everything in my power to shut him down. If I succeed, I'll go wherever you are. And in the meantime, there won't be anyone else for me. I'm playing the long game here, Madeleina."

"Me, too."

We kissed, sealing the promise.

He held me for a long time. I felt so perfectly happy in his arms. Maybe if I didn't move, we could always stay like this. And I could keep all of my fears at bay.

But eventually, he stirred. "Are you hungry? Thought we'd head out for dinner."

"You want to wine and dine me?"

"Dine you, at least," he said with a smile. "Can't order wine where I'm taking you. They'd probably check ID."

"How old are you, anyway?"

"Nineteen and three quarters."

I laughed. Then the buzzer went off, startling us both.

Ortiz went over to press the intercom. "Yeah?"

"It's X."

"C'mon up." He looked at me apologetically. "If it's not important I'll throw his ass out of here."

"No worries," I said, smoothing my clothing.

Seconds later, X's broad, athletic frame darkened the doorway. He pounded fists with Ortiz, stopping short when he saw me. A smile came to his lips, but he quickly put it away. "Hi, Maddie."

"Hey, X."

He turned to Ortiz. "Don't mean to interrupt. Got a minute?"

"Of course."

X helped himself to a soda from the fridge and sat down at the kitchen table, as if he'd done it a hundred times before. Ortiz joined him. I figured it was best if I kept my distance and let them talk, so I stayed on the futon.

"Found her," X said. "Miami Gardens. I spent the last couple of nights doing my sketches on the main drag. Talked to a guy who knew a guy."

"Reyes?"

"Yeah. Name's Sergio. He has her walk the streets and tails her in an SUV. He's got two or three girls out there at the same time."

"Snatch-up?"

X nodded. "I'm picking Rubio up in twenty minutes. He'll grab her, then we'll drive her out to her parents'."

"Think she'll go quietly?"

"She wants to go home, trust me."

I wondered how X could know that, but Ortiz didn't question him. They seemed to understand each other beyond words.

I glanced at the artwork on the wall and back at X. He was a paradox if I'd ever seen one. He looked like a tough-as-nails jock, but he created beautiful art. And he was putting his energy into helping girls he'd never met. I understood why Ortiz did it, but what about him?

X got up and went to the door. "Later, Lobo. Maddie." And then he was gone. Ortiz came over to me. "He calls these things like a pro. It'll go well."

"You don't need to go with them?"

He shook his head. "A snatch-up is a two person job. X is in charge of this one."

"How'd you find out about this girl?"

"She ran away from home four months ago. Was really messed up by her parents' divorce. Her family's been all over Miami with flyers. X got one from her father."

"So X uses his street art as a way to watch what's going on out there? Seems like an interesting guy. I'd love to know his story."

"I wish I could tell you, but it's his story, not mine. You could ask him sometime."

"I don't want to pry. Just tell me one thing: why does he call himself X?"

Ortiz gave a grudging smile. "That's how I know you're a great reporter. You ask the only question worth asking."

GONE

Boyd signed the papers. Hallelujah!

"What's making you smile like that?" Iz asked, drowning her chef's salad in dressing. "Did Ortiz send you a selfie?"

"The divorce is final." I closed my eyes, taking it in. It was really over. The deed was done, the goods were split, and most important, Dex was ours.

Iz side-hugged me. "Hooray!"

"Maybe I'll make Mom a special drink for the occasion: a Divorcée's Daiquiri?"

Iz looked over my shoulder as I texted Mom back.

I'm taking you out for dinner to celebrate!

"Wanna come with?" I asked her.

"I thought you were seeing your man tonight."

"Not till later. Come on, it'll be fun."

"Can't. Eric and Julia are coming over."

My mouth fell open. "Julia, too? Was it a package deal?"

She sighed. "Look, I'm not her biggest fan, but I know I was a bitch to her and I'm trying to make amends. Besides, Eric made me invite her."

I smirked. "I thought you didn't take orders from a guy."

"He's blood. And he's always stood by me. So I'm gonna make an effort with Julia. Now, where are you taking your mom?"

"I have to figure that out. Somewhere with good-looking men where she can be excited to be single."

"You have to choose the right place, then," she said between crunches of salad. "What type of guy is she into?"

"She's done with losers. Anything else she's open to."

Iz put down her fork and picked up her phone. "I'm texting Aunt Maria. She *knows* the single scene, honey."

Iz's aunt got back to her within minutes with a list of suggestions, organized by types of men. For slick businessmen and hardnosed lawyers, Juanita's. For working-class sports fans, Raoul's Crab Shack. For the wealthy South Beach business owners, try the Town Grill. In the end, I chose Raoul's. Mom didn't need a guy who thought he was hot shit. She needed a kind, reliable guy who could put in an honest day's work.

Raoul's Crab Shack was a Cuban restaurant with a bustling patio. Iz's aunt Maria was right on—there were lots of ringless men around, some of them still carrying their orange construction vests. As Mom sipped her mojito, she glanced at the men with interest, which gave me hope.

I tried to convince her to go up to the bar to order a drink, but she said that would be too obvious. I bet she would have if she had another drink in her and were here with a girlfriend, not me.

Even though I wasn't drinking, I was borderline giddy, and so was she. We laughed like we hadn't laughed in a long time. The weight of Boyd had been lifted from us. The best part was that we didn't even mention his name. It was as if we'd both agreed that he didn't deserve one more moment of our time. We'd given him enough already.

After dinner, Mom and I got in separate cabs—Mom's heading for home, mine heading for Ortiz's. I had a feeling she was going home to start a profile on a dating website, something I'd been trying to convince her to do for months.

Ortiz wasn't waiting for me outside, since I was twenty minutes early. I buzzed his apartment, but there was no answer, so I sat on the front step and sent him a text. It was Wednesday night, so he was probably boxing with Eric at the gym. I wasn't comfortable sitting there, though, and it had nothing to do with the hard concrete step under my butt. The neighborhood was beyond sketchy. Shady men walked by, eyeing me with a little too much interest. Stick-thin girls cruised the street looking for johns.

As the minutes passed, I started to wonder if he'd forgotten that I was coming over. I texted him again and waited.

When a female resident left the building, I caught the door behind her. I debated getting into the elevator, but decided not to. It was the old, tiny type that I wouldn't risk without a day's supply of food and water. So I walked up the four flights of stairs instead.

As I approached the door to his apartment, I noticed that it was slightly open.

A feeling of dread rolled over me.

Ortiz always double-locked the door. True, he'd been expecting me. But he couldn't have thought I'd get into the building without him answering the buzzer.

My instincts were going off like a smoke alarm. I knew what Ortiz would say to do in this situation: *Get out of there.*

But I couldn't do that.

My heart thudded in my chest as I eased the door open. I walked in, careful not to make a sound on the hardwood.

I held my breath.

It looked like a tornado had blown through the room. There were splatters of blood on the floor.

He was gone.

I felt my knees buckle.

They'd taken him.

BLOOD

THERE WAS NO TIME TO BREAK DOWN. I had to think.

Ortiz was alive. He had to be. And that meant I could still help him.

X. I had to call X.

His number was already in my phone. Because I'd been afraid of this.

I called the number. It rang and rang and—

"Who's this?" X answered. He sounded like he was in his car.

"It's Maddie. I'm at Lobo's. He's gone. And there's blood."

"Wait there. I'm ten minutes away." He hung up.

X was coming. That was good.

I slowly moved around the apartment. Shock, I realized,

was when you kept the emotions at bay and functioned anyway. The futon was opened into a bed, and messy, as if he'd been sleeping when they came. His laptop was upside down on the floor. In the struggle, someone must've slammed into the bookshelf, because books were scattered all over the place.

X appeared minutes later. He scanned the room. "I'm going to the safe house. You'd better come with me."

We flew down the stairs to his car. He floored the gas. He drove so fast I had to work against its momentum to put on my seat belt.

"Is there someone I can call at the safe house—to warn them?" I asked.

"I called," he said. "No one's answering."

"Oh my God. What do you think is happening?"

"I think we're in trouble."

X drove scary fast, and yet he had total control, maneuvering the car like it was an extension of himself. He also knew the right places to slow down, where cops were waiting for speeders.

"We're gonna get to Ortiz, but I need you to think," he said. "There's been a leak somewhere. And our best chance at finding Ortiz in time is to trace back where it came from."

It took me a second to register that he thought the leak came through me. That was why he'd taken me with him, I realized.

"I didn't tell anyone about him. I would never risk it."

"Someone must've suspected."

My stomach fell. Oh my God, could it be?

"My friend Iz suspected," I told him. "But I can't believe she'd tell anyone."

"Call her."

I did.

She answered, "Hey Maddie, what's up?"

"Iz, listen to me. I need to ask you something very important. You know how you wondered if Ortiz was Lobo? I need to know if you told anyone."

"What? What are you—Eric, turn it down for a sec. It's Maddie and she's freaking out about something. Sorry, what?"

"You must've told someone that you thought Ortiz was Lobo," I said. "Who did you tell?"

"Huh? I didn't tell anyone. What's happening, Maddie? Is Ortiz in trouble?"

"*Think*, Iz, for fuck's sake. Who did you tell?"

"I told you, I didn't tell anyone. You'd have to be crazy to spread a rumor like that! Wait a minute—are you saying I was *right*?"

"No. Someone just got the wrong idea about him. Gotta go."

I hung up. "It wasn't her."

"You sure about that?"

"Yeah." Iz wasn't the leak, I was positive. Even though we'd had our problems, she wouldn't have betrayed my secret about Lobo helping me the night of the attack. And she never would've started a rumor about Ortiz knowing it could get him killed.

When we got to the safe house, X ran inside. I hurried in after him, through the door and down the stairs, and stopped dead.

X was bent over Rubio, who was crumpled on the floor. A pool of blood spread out under him.

Kelsey was curled up on the couch, sobbing. I went to her.

"Are you okay, Kelsey? What happened?"

"He h-held them off while Felix got the girls out." Her lip was bloodied and half of her face was swollen. "They sh-shot him." She balled herself up tighter, tucking her head into her knees.

"We'll get you to a hospital," I told her. "You'll be all right."

X stood up, staring down at Rubio. He looked at me, and I knew that Rubio was dead.

"Paramedics are on their way," he said, putting away his phone. "They'll take care of her. We need to go talk to your friend, Manny Soto."

"Manny? But—"

"He used to be one of Salazar's guys." His blue eyes were icy. "He's our best chance at finding Ortiz."

* * *

Minutes later, we pulled up in front of Manny's house.

X said, "I'll stay here. Bring him outside. Make him think you're alone."

I hesitated. X didn't plan to hurt Manny, did he? Of course not. X knew that we needed Manny's help to find Ortiz. "All right."

I rang the doorbell. A hairy man in a wifebeater answered the door. "Hey mamacita. You here for my boy?"

I nodded. "I need to talk to him."

The man called out, "Manuel, a girlie is here!"

Manny came bounding down the stairs in a T-shirt and shorts. He looked more like a gangly teen than an ex-con. Not at all like someone who'd once been in the Reyes.

Manny could tell something was wrong. It wasn't like I'd ever showed up at his place before. "What's going on?"

"Let's talk outside."

We went out to the porch. The night air was humid, suffocating, like a wet blanket.

"Ortiz was taken by the Reyes."

Manny's eyes went big. "Why? What'd he do?"

"He's Lobo, the head of the Destinos."

His mouth opened in shock. "You've gotta be . . ." He didn't bother to finish.

"I need to find out where he is. I know you were one of them once."

Manny didn't deny it. "If your boyfriend is Lobo . . ." He was shaking his head. "God, I'm sorry. I really am. But there's nothing you can do for him."

"*Don't*," I snapped. "Don't act like he's dead already."

Manny plunked down on a chair, head in his hands. "He might not be. But it would take the national guard to get to him. I don't know how many Destinos there are, but they wouldn't have a prayer of getting him out."

"So you know where Salazar's holding him."

"Yeah, that's how I know it's impossible. Anyone who goes in is not coming out. I know Salazar and his guys, Diaz. They're evil."

"I don't care what they are. We're going to get Ortiz out of there."

His head shot up. "Well, you fucking *should* care. They won't take pity on you because you're a girl. I can't let you walk into that."

"Then let *me* walk into it," said another voice. X emerged from the shadows, holding a switchblade. "You have five seconds before I shove this under your ribs."

Manny didn't seem afraid. "Not if you're taking her with you." There was a hollow, inevitable note in his voice.

"I won't take her with me," X said. "I don't need her. What I need is a location." He took several steps closer to Manny. "Five, four, three . . ."

X was bluffing. He had to be. But as he stalked toward Manny, suddenly I wasn't so sure. "X, stop it. He's going to help us. Right, Manny?"

"Fuck." Manny rubbed a hand over his face. "It's Brown's Airport. There's a warehouse. Salazar's been holing up there the past couple months. It used to store airplane parts and shit but it's been abandoned since the nineties. The place is like a fortress. He's been using it on and off for years."

"Are you sure about this?" I asked.

Manny nodded. "I stay informed. Still got buddies who are Reyes."

I looked at X. "We'll pick up Felix and . . ."

"No," X said, cutting me off. "Your friend's right about one thing. It's not a job we can do. We don't have an arsenal of machine guns. There's only one person who can help us."

I didn't know who he meant, but Manny did, because he barked a laugh. "Good fucking luck. His guys will slit your throat before you even get near him."

"But they won't slit hers," X countered.

Manny's eyes bugged out. "You said you'd keep her out of it!"

"It's the only way. If he'll trust anyone, it'll be her."

Manny jumped to his feet, advancing on X. "I'll kill you."

X shrugged. "Trust me, Soto. If anything happens to her, Ortiz will do it for you."

"What are we talking about?" I demanded.

"El Chueco," Manny said tightly. "Your Destino friend here wants to feed you to the lion."

El Chueco. The head of the cartel.

It took me several seconds to process it. Now that we knew Salazar's location, we could give El Chueco what he wanted most: a chance to kill Salazar.

"I'll do it," I said without hesitation. "I'll go to him."

"So your plan is to stroll up to El Chueco and try to cut a deal with him?" Manny said, incredulous. "El Chueco could do *worse* than kill you. Don't you get that?"

"El Chueco has four daughters," X said. "Word is he has a soft spot for women. He mostly keeps them out of the line of fire."

"A cartel head with a code?" Manny said. "You've got to be kidding. Maddie, you want to take that risk?"

"Yes." I'd risk whatever I had to for Ortiz. "Do you know where to find him?" I asked X.

He nodded. "Let's go."

As we headed to the car, Manny ran after us, grabbing my arm. I thought it was to pull me away, but instead he went in front of me, sliding into the backseat. "I'm coming with you."

CROOKED

DON'T THINK. DON'T FEAR. JUST SURVIVE THIS. For Ortiz.

I had to focus on one thing: the moment I'd have him in my arms again. Nothing between this moment and then mattered.

X drove, a maestro of the roads. He knew where he was going and it took him all of twenty minutes to get there. The city lights were long behind us.

We came to the Palmeras, a glitzy resort with tall fountains shooting up from an enormous blue pool. It was the cream of the industry, Mom had once told me, the only six-star hotel this side of the Atlantic. I wondered if the owners knew they were favored by a Mexican cartel.

"High security here. Valet parking. I have to drop you off."

X pulled to the side of the road a few yards from the entrance. It was a huge archway that reminded me of MGM Studios.

"We'll wait for you here," X said. "Now go to the front desk and ask for Mr. Crooks. He'll send someone down. That's when you'll have to make your case to see him."

"What am I going to say to El Chueco?" Between the pounding of my heart and the engine of the car, I wasn't sure I'd hear his answer.

"Tell him the truth. Don't lie. If you lie, he'll smell it."

"I'm going in with her," Manny said from the backseat.

X threw him a *don't fuck with me* glare. "Yeah, a former Reyes. One of his men could recognize you."

Manny seethed. "Then you go with her."

"I wish I could, but there's no chance he would trust me." X turned my way. "Tell him who you are, Maddie—that you're the witness. Tell him about Ortiz and the Destinos. And tell him that he owes us a favor."

I nodded. Tell a cartel head that he owes us. Right.

"What favor are we talking about?"

"We rescued a couple of girls from his village a few months ago. Cousins of his. El Chueco knows what we did for them. It should get you in the door."

"And if he isn't there?"

"Then he's probably close by. This is where I dropped off his cousins—they told me he goes by the name Crooks. Guess he has a sense of humor. I've been keeping an eye on the place ever since, and I've seen his men coming and going."

"Okay." As I got out of the car, I caught a flash of X's face in the car light. It was a *you will do this* look. Then I caught a glimpse of the fear in Manny's eyes, and slammed the door.

I walked through the archway, my knees trembling. I had a sudden memory of being twelve years old and having to dive off the three-meter springboard. I'd gone up there on a dare, nervous but determined to do it. But the second I'd looked down, I was lost. I'd stretched my arms out hesitantly, not fully committing to the dive, and did a painful and humiliating belly flop.

I had to commit to this, I realized. There was no other option. No running away, no screwing it up halfway through. Ortiz's life—and mine—were on the line.

The lobby of the hotel was a white marble palace, its ceilings vaulted like the Vatican. Huge crystal chandeliers dangled over the elegantly dressed guests.

The front desk was a long marble counter that seemed to be floating in the middle of the room. A male staff member in a maroon suit greeted me with a smile.

"Hi, I'm here to see to Mr. Crooks," I said.

The man blinked, my only clue that this was not a normal request, but his smile stayed put. "Sorry, ma'am, you said Mr. . . ."

"Crooks."

"Crooks. Thank you, ma'am." Although he was extremely subtle about it, I could tell he was looking me over. I wore black jeans, ballet flats, and a white tank top with a picture of a black rose on it. Though I wasn't all done up, he'd probably still conclude I was a prostitute.

"I will call Mr. Crooks's room. Kindly give me a minute." Instead of using the company phone, he took out his cell. He stepped away from the desk and spoke very quietly. The conversation seemed to last forever. Finally, he returned. "Someone will come and meet you. Won't be long."

"Awesome, thanks."

I tapped my foot as I waited, trying to stand up straight and keep a sunny look on my face. Trying not to reveal that I was terrified.

Ortiz. Focus on Ortiz. Nothing else.

A minute later, a big Mexican man in a suit came out of the elevator and headed straight for me. He gestured to the corner of the room beside a small palm tree.

"*¿Quién es?*" he asked.

"Maddie Diaz. Sorry, my Spanish isn't very good. I need to speak to El Chueco."

That was my first risk, calling his boss by his real name. The big man didn't flinch. "He's not expecting another girl tonight," he said in English.

"That's not why I'm here. I'm here for the Destinos." I cleared my throat, trying to push out a strong voice. "I can help him find Salazar."

The man glared at me, his dark eyebrows slashing together. It hit me that this man had probably killed on El Chueco's behalf without hesitation or remorse. And now he was assessing what, if any, threat I posed to his boss.

"Tell El Chueco he owes the Destinos for helping his cousins, and I'm here to collect."

The man didn't look impressed by my show of bravery. Maybe it was because my voice broke on the word *collect*.

"Come." He grabbed my arm, a little too tightly, and brought me to wait for the elevator. The doors opened.

In the elevator, he released my arm and pressed a button for the twelfth floor. The elevator shot up quickly, the floor lurching below us. When the doors opened, we stepped into an opulent, too bright hallway lined with huge sconces. There were two security suits stationed in the hallway.

They surrounded me and frisked me thoroughly. I didn't care; I spread my arms and legs to make it easier for them. My purse was snatched away and one of them went through it, examining my driver's license. I told myself this had to be a good sign. They wouldn't be scrutinizing me if they didn't intend to let me see El Chueco, would they?

When they were finished, one of the suits led me into a

room and left me there, closing the door behind him.

It wasn't your typical hotel room. Pure white, with gold accents and a massive four-poster bed. There was no luggage, so I doubted anyone was staying in here. I bet El Chueco had rented the whole floor.

I breathed, slowly and steadily. Any second now, El Chueco could walk into the room. What would I say? So many possibilities flooded my head that I was afraid they would fall out in a jumble and he'd send me away.

My name is Maddie Diaz. I'm the witness who's going to testify against two Reyes for killing that homeless man. I'm a friend of the Destinos gang. We can help you get Salazar.

Minutes passed and no one came. Eventually I sat down on a plush couch. It was just after ten. I should contact Mom while I had the chance.

My fingers shook as I texted her.

A friend needs me right now. I will be very late. Don't wait up. I love you, Mom.

I'd added the "I love you" just in case. Just in case this was the last text I ever sent.

As the minutes ticked by, my optimism about seeing El Chueco was starting to die. What if El Chueco's men had no intention of letting me speak to him? What if they were keeping me here for some other reason?

I pushed those thoughts aside, and turned them back to Mom. I could imagine her cursing as she read my text, making plans to ground me until I went off to college. I'd gladly accept being grounded if it meant I survived tonight—and if it meant Ortiz survived.

The thought of him almost undid me. I refused to believe that he could be dead. I couldn't even go there. But I knew he must be suffering. Suffering at the hands of Salazar.

Oh, God.

My stomach lurched and I ran to the bathroom, dry-heaving over the toilet. My own situation, I could handle. But to know that Ortiz could be fighting for his life right now . . . I couldn't bear it.

Ortiz had always known this day could come. That was why he'd written the note.

. . . just so you never doubt it. I love you and always will.

I should've told him I'd read the note. Should've told him that I loved him too. A wave of grief crashed over me, but I didn't allow myself to break down. Instead I asked myself what he'd say to me if he were here.

The answer popped into my head. *Don't count me out yet, Madeleina.*

He'd want me to get it together. To be strong.

Slowly I got up and went over to the couch. I had to find a

still place inside me. I remembered the night we'd walked on the beach. Before he had told me about his past, he'd held my hand, and we hadn't needed words. I clung to that memory, to the happiness I'd known in those moments. I could almost feel the wind whipping my hair, hear the rhythm of the waves.

I walked around the room, touching the painting on the wall, the television remote control, the lamps, trying to ground myself in the present.

The door opened. I turned around calmly. Three black suits walked in with a heavyset, scar-faced guy in his forties. Though he wore jeans and a loose black T-shirt, he exuded authority.

"What is *this*?" El Chueco asked, narrowing his eyes.

This, I figured, meant *me*. "I'm Maddie Diaz. I'm the witness who—"

He flicked a hand, silencing me. "I know who you are. What you want?"

Slow and steady, I coached myself. "I'm here because of Lobo, the head of the Destinos. Salazar kidnapped him. I know where he's being held. And I need your help to get him out. I can lead you to Salazar."

His chin hiked. "How can you promise me Salazar will be there?"

"Salazar hates Lobo. He wants to be the one to hurt him. Do you think he'd be anywhere else? Would *you*?" I wanted him to think of his own enemies and what *he* would do when he got his hands on them.

El Chueco didn't answer me. "Where's his hideout, then?"

I hesitated. "So you're going to help us?"

"I asked you," he repeated slowly, "where is Salazar's hideout?"

He moved a step closer. I stood my ground. El Chueco wasn't used to being questioned and wouldn't allow anyone to hold out on him. But I had to bank on X's view that he didn't go after women the way he did men.

I took a breath. "He's hiding out in a warehouse outside the city. But I need you to promise you'll help us before I tell you where."

He scrutinized me, like a scientist who didn't know what type of specimen he was looking at. "Tell me how you know about this warehouse."

I remembered what X had told me—*don't lie, or he'll smell it.* "My friend used to be in the Reyes and he still has connections. He knows where Salazar's hideout is."

El Chueco's face morphed into a smile. He snapped his fingers.

The door swung open and Manny was dragged in. He'd been beaten, and was gasping for breath. "This your friend? We found him hanging around."

Manny's shirt was ripped open, revealing the *R* tattoo on his chest.

"Sorry," Manny uttered before taking a punch in the face.

Trust Manny to play the hero and go in after me. If I hadn't admitted I had a friend in the Reyes, El Chueco might have killed us both.

"That's him," I said coolly. "He's not in the Reyes anymore. He wants to see Salazar go down as much as I do."

"You know what we do to Reyes?" El Chueco taunted me.

I wasn't sure if I was supposed to answer or not, but I couldn't risk silence. "The mark of death?"

"No, señorita. Only death." He snapped his fingers again, and one of the suits put a gun to Manny's head.

I froze.

"You think you can come here and lead me into an ambush?" El Chueco spit out. "You think I'm *estupido*?"

"No!" I said, putting my hands out in a plea. "I know you're way too smart for that. And you're too smart to give up a chance to get Salazar. If you kill my friend, you've lost your chance. He's the only one who knows the exact location of the warehouse and the best way in."

El Chueco flicked his hand. I squeezed my eyes shut, but there was no gunshot. When I opened them, the goon had lowered his gun.

"All right, señorita." El Chueco's smile was scary as he

turned to his men. "Let's have some fun, eh?"

The men nodded, lips curling.

El Chueco walked up to me until his face was inches from mine. "You and your Reyes friend are gonna lead my men into this warehouse." I could practically taste the smoke and liquor on his breath. "Something goes wrong, we kill you on the spot. What you say to that, little señorita?"

"I say let's do this."

THE RAID

AT 11:37 P.M., WE WERE DRIVING DOWN a dark highway.

Manny and I sat hunched together in the back of a van with six of El Chueco's men. Six goons whose mission it was to find Salazar. Six goons who didn't give a shit about rescuing Ortiz—and who wouldn't hesitate to kill us if they thought they'd been set up.

If Manny was wrong about this warehouse, we were both screwed. And if Salazar wasn't there, it was all over for us. But Manny was convinced that he was right.

"There are usually two guards at the back door," Manny told Nino, the security guy I'd met in the hotel lobby. "Salazar hangs out in one of the top floor offices. We check there first."

Nino gave instructions to his men in Spanish, then called

the other van full of El Chueco's men. It all felt surreal, like we were part of a SWAT team on some TV show.

Manny turned to face me. "Ortiz will be down below, in the basement. That's where Salazar holds people. When we get inside, go to the first stairwell on the left and go down as far as you can. They have these huge storage lockers for airplane parts. Search them. It's a maze down there, so it could take some time. If anyone's with him, stay back and wait for us. Got it?"

"Got it." I wished Manny could come with me, but he had to stay with El Chueco's men to help them find Salazar. Once that was done, I could count on their help to rescue Ortiz. That was our deal.

Suddenly I heard the clicks of machine guns all around us—the clicks of the safeties being removed.

Nino gave the order, and the van surged forward, barreling toward the warehouse. I held on to my seat. The van stopped, and men rushed out, opening fire on the guards at the back door. Manny and I hung back until the way was clear. Once all of the men had disappeared inside, we went in.

Shouting and gunfire echoed through the hallways, blasting my ears.

"That way," Manny shouted to me, pushing me toward a steel door. "Go down all the way. Go!"

I ran down the stairs and swung open another door. I

found myself in a long, gray hallway with storage lockers on either side. I moved forward, glancing inside each one. Empty. Above me, I heard the shrill sounds of gunfire as El Chueco's men engaged the Reyes.

I went down the rest of the hallway, careful not to make noise. *Where the hell is Ortiz?* I found another door and a connecting hallway with more storage spaces. Nothing. The place was completely empty. There was no sign of Ortiz, or of anyone having been down here recently.

A cold feeling gripped me. If Manny was wrong about Ortiz being down here, what else was he wrong about?

Had Ortiz been here at all? Was he already . . . ?

The sound of people running vibrated the floor above me. Gunfire erupted again, reaching a deafening pitch. I hoped Manny was staying back, out of the crossfire.

Oh my God. Manny didn't send me down here to find Ortiz. He sent me down here to keep me safe.

Suddenly the gunfire stopped.

I had to go upstairs. If Ortiz was in this warehouse, that was where he would be.

Running up several flights of stairs, I opened a heavy door and caught my breath. Four dead bodies sprawled on the ground. They were all Reyes, since they weren't wearing the black gear of El Chueco's goons.

The smell of blood filled my nostrils, and a wave of

nausea came over me. But I kept going, trying not to look at the bodies.

I heard agonized screaming from farther down the hallway.

Turning a corner, I came face-to-face with four of El Chueco's goons. There were two more bodies on the ground in front of them.

I spotted Nino. "Where's—" But my words got cut off by a horrific scream.

Manny came out of the next room, carrying a body over his shoulder. A body whose clothes were bloody, in shreds.

It was Ortiz.

My heart stopped.

"He's alive," Manny said, breathing hard. He kept moving, heading down the hallway, carrying Ortiz's limp body while stepping over bodies and guns.

Alive. Ortiz was alive.

Another agonized scream. It came from the same room he'd dragged Ortiz from.

"Is that Salazar?" I asked.

"Yeah," Manny said through gritted teeth. "And it's just what the motherfucker deserves."

Right before we reached the back door of the warehouse, it swung open. X stood there. "Let me take him."

X propped Ortiz on his shoulder, then maneuvered him into his car. Ortiz crumpled into the backseat, and I slid in beside him. Manny and X jumped in front and X hit the gas, taking us from zero to seventy in seconds.

I propped Ortiz's head on my lap, tilting it up so he wouldn't choke on his own blood. The sight of his messed-up, swollen face was horrifying. I grabbed a blanket and put it over him.

I flashed back to a moment when the situation had been reversed—when Ortiz had cradled me in his lap after I'd been attacked. I'd been hurt, bloody, traumatized. He was a stranger then, but he had been able to comfort me. He'd told me that I would be fine, and I had believed him.

"Helluva night, huh?" I said, echoing his words of that night. His eyes were closed, but I hoped that he could hear me. "Don't worry. You're gonna be fine." I fought to keep the tears out of my voice. "I've got you."

AWAKE

I WOULD NEVER FORGET HEARING THE DOCTORS gasp when they cut open Ortiz's clothes. The trauma unit usually saw victims of car wrecks and construction accidents. Not torture.

But Ortiz was a survivor. Over the next few hours, X kept reminding me of that. And he was right. Ortiz would get through this. *We* would get through this.

The hospital staff wanted to contact his family. X and I explained that we were his family, and that we had no intention of leaving his side. We took turns holding his hand. Sometimes he'd make sounds in his sleep, a piercing cry or a terrible groan.

I texted my mom.

I'm at University of Miami Hospital. Ortiz got beaten up
and I'm staying with him tonight. He was sticking up for
someone who needed help. I'm proud of him.

It was all I could tell her for now, maybe for a long time
yet. There were still Reyes out there, and still Destinos to
protect.

Ortiz woke up the next evening. His eyes opened, blood
red with burst vessels. He grabbed my hand and said, "Kelsey."

X and I exchanged a worried look. The doctor had warned
us that Ortiz could be confused when he woke up. But it had
never occurred to me that he wouldn't recognize me.

"No, it's me, Madeleina," I said gently. "You're at the hospital. You're safe."

Ortiz's mouth was puffy, but he repeated, "Kelsey."

"She's out of the hospital now," X assured him. "Wasn't
hurt bad. Said she was going back to her family."

"No." Ortiz's hand gripped mine tightly. "It was *her*."

Before I could vocalize my shock, X said, "Kelsey was the
leak? Is that what you're saying?"

"Yeah." Ortiz eased back into the pillow, relieved to have
conveyed his message.

"God damn her!" X said.

Ortiz swallowed, and I could see even that movement
caused him pain. "What about . . . everyone?"

I glanced at X. We'd decided not to tell him about Rubio's death, not until he was stronger. But I wavered. I didn't think Ortiz would believe us if we lied.

X answered, "The safe house was attacked. Felix and Rubio were there. Felix got the girls out in time." He glanced at me, unsure of what to say next.

"And Rubio?" After a few beats of silence, Ortiz turned away from us and squeezed his eyes shut. "Fuck."

"It was a bullet, Lobo," X said. "Quick. He didn't suffer."

Ortiz took a ragged breath, his eyes still closed. But when he opened them again, they glistened with tears.

"I can't believe Kelsey turned on you. Doesn't make any sense." But even as I said it, something niggled at my brain. Hadn't Kelsey told me that loving Salazar had been her addiction? It hadn't occurred to me that she had still been struggling with it.

"She was still in love with Salazar," I said. "That's why."

Ortiz gave a weak nod. "He said she begged him to take her back."

"And sold us all out." X's rage rippled through the room.

"She gave me up, no one else," Ortiz said. "But Salazar's guys tailed her, found the safe house."

X was incredulous. "Kelsey thought she could trust Salazar? She was delusional. She must've known what he'd do to you."

"She knew," Ortiz said. "I'm the one she hates."

I didn't understand. "Why? You're the one who rescued her."

Ortiz looked at me through bloodshot eyes. "That's why. She never wanted to be rescued. She wanted to die."

It took several moments for that to sink in. Kelsey had wanted to destroy herself—maybe as a sign of her love for Salazar. Ortiz had forced her to survive, but he hadn't been able to heal her.

"Kelsey will have to live with what she did, or die with it," X said. "Salazar is dead. Her gamble left her fucked."

"But we got him." Ortiz's swollen mouth tried to smile. "You got him, X."

X shook his head. "I can't take the credit, Lobo. It was El Chueco who killed him."

Ortiz stared at him. "El Chueco?"

"Your girlfriend called in a favor." X gave me an admiring look. "You're a tough bitch, Maddie Diaz. No offense."

"None taken."

Ortiz turned to me in amazement. I lifted his bruised hand and brought it to my lips. "You're the one who said I had the alpha in me."

Two weeks later, I was lying on his bed, gazing up at him. Ortiz was propped up on one elbow, his finger tracing a freckle on my chest. "I love you, Madeleina."

He'd said it a hundred times already, and I'd said it a hundred times back. I couldn't help but think that if the world consisted of nothing but me and Ortiz, I would be happy forever.

But it didn't. There was a darkness, an ugliness beyond this bed and this room. We'd both seen it firsthand. And yet, somehow, it made us feel all the more lucky to be alive, and to have found each other.

We kissed, long and slow. Ortiz's recovery had wowed everyone, especially the doctors, but he still had a ways to go. He looked like the survivor of a car wreck. His arm was in a cast, broken in several places. His face and body bore the marks of Salazar's cruelty, and maybe always would. It didn't matter. I'd love each scar, each burn, and take his hurt as my own. And hopefully my love could heal the wounds that time wouldn't erase.

Ortiz had told me that if El Chueco's men hadn't stormed the building when they had, he would've been dead within minutes. He said he was lucky that Salazar had insisted on hurting him first, on pounding into his head how stupid he'd been to fuck with him.

Hours after Ortiz's rescue, Salazar's body had been found on the side of a highway near the warehouse. El Chueco could easily have made the body disappear, but he wanted to make headlines. His message to Miami: *I won.*

The new power of the cartel was no comfort to me. But Salazar would never hurt anyone ever again. And, from the word on the street, his trafficking business was crumbling.

Ortiz pulled back from the kiss, cradling my cheek. "I gave my landlord notice today."

"Does that mean you're coming with me to Tallahassee?"

"Of course. That's always been the plan." He raised an eyebrow. "You weren't sure?"

"I was hoping but . . . I didn't want to pressure you."

"You haven't pressured me." He was achingly beautiful when he smiled, even with the cuts and bruises that lingered on his face.

Our hands clasped together. "It's strange, you know," he said. "I feel . . . happy. I don't think I've been happy for a long time."

I knew that was true. He'd never felt that he deserved to be happy after what had happened to his sister.

"Andrea would be happy too," I said.

I saw the emotion in his eyes. "I know."

We kissed again. When he finally pulled back, he said, "X doesn't want me to move on."

I frowned. "But Salazar's dead. And the Reyes can't hold it together without him. You said it yourself."

"Salazar isn't the only trafficker out there. X is determined to keep going. The others are in too."

That caught me off guard. I'd assumed that when Ortiz called it quits, the Destinos would disband. "Don't they need you as a leader?"

"X can lead. It's in him. I can't tell them to stop. It's their choice."

"I've seen how loyal they are to you, especially X. He wouldn't leave your side in the hospital. I can't believe he doesn't understand why you need to move on."

"He understands, all right. He just doesn't like it." His eyes darkened. "Salazar was my demon, Madeleina. And he's dead now. But X, he has demons of his own. And they're not going to disappear anytime soon."

Two exams down, one to go.

I sat at Café Varadero the following week, sipping my coffee and people-watching. Tomorrow's exam was English, and I was mostly prepared. I went over some of my class notes, watching the door for Julia.

She breezed in, looking chic and writerly in a white gauze dress and yellow belt. She hugged me tight. "How's it going? How's Ortiz?"

"I'm good. He's stubborn as hell. He's at physio right now working his legs."

"He'd better keep at it. Eric says he challenged him to a

fight next month—with one arm tied behind their backs."

I rolled my eyes. "Eric could beat him senseless by using his cast against him. Hey, I have something to show you. Found it this morning." I reached into my bag and pulled out a section of the *Miami Herald*.

Her eyes widened. "They published your letter to the editor!"

I nodded. "Look at that picture of Hector."

She held the paper in front of her. It was a young, bare-chested Hector on the beach, his arm slung around his sister. Pure happiness.

As Julia stared at the picture, her eyes filled with tears. "Good stuff, girl."

"Thanks to you. The info from his sister's page was really helpful. I'll forward you a copy to send to her in case she hasn't seen it yet." I slid my laptop in front of her. "Check this out. There are more than fifty comments so far. People *got* it."

I scrolled down so she could see the latest comments.

"Wise words from a high school student. Good to see the next generation isn't as ignorant as ours."

"Too bad our mayor's so focused on tourism that he doesn't give a damn about hard-done-by people like Hector Rodriguez."

"Hector was a kind soul."

Julia raised her eyes. "It's not a coincidence that you were there to witness what happened to him that night. That you wrote this tribute for him." She looked skyward. "Rest in peace, Hector."

"I'm not sure if he can rest in peace yet." In my mind, the calendar was flipping ahead. "I'll be there to speak for him at the trial next summer. And hopefully once his killers are convicted, *then* he can rest in peace."

BRING IT ON

I GOT OUT OF THE LIMO IN A TOO-TIGHT, too-short black dress, careful not to give anyone a peek of my panties. But that's what you get when you buy a dress off the rack two days before prom and don't have time to have it fitted to your measurements.

I couldn't believe I was here. I'd had no intention of going to prom, not with Ortiz still laid up at home. But he had encouraged me to go, and Iz wouldn't take no for an answer.

"I'm going to hire a transporter to throw your ass in a van," Iz had threatened. "Trust me, you don't want that to happen. Because he'd drop you off on the dance floor in a T-shirt and shorts while the rest of us are looking stunning."

So here I was, with Abby by my side. She'd gone to her

own prom last week, and I'd had no trouble getting her to come along tonight.

As we entered the gymnasium, I was amazed at how the prom committee had transformed the place. It was a picture of white frilliness, from the long, white curtain backdrop to white bows everywhere. Although some pops of pink had been added in, it was all very weddingy. Then I remembered hearing that Miss Kemp, who had gotten married last weekend, had donated her decorations to the prom committee.

We were lucky to have a prom at all. Last year, a group of idiot jocks had gone crazy and trashed a hotel banquet hall, bringing on thousands in fines and clean-up costs. So the admin had decided to keep it at the school this year. Go figure. "Wonder who's getting married." Abby frowned as she scanned the set up.

"Iz and Rob, by the looks of it," I said. They were smoking hot on the dance floor. Although they weren't officially back together yet, it wouldn't be long now. Rob was still hung up on her, and Iz had gained a new appreciation for him after he'd dumped her. It probably wouldn't last, but who knew?

"You look amazing," I said to Abby. "Let's send Kyle another pic." I reached out for her phone. "Here, let's get one with the white backdrop behind you. Something sexy, for Kyle's fantasies. A boudoir photo."

Abby struck a mock-sexy pose, lips pouting.

Click. "Ha!" I showed her the picture.

She glanced at the photo, giggled, and sent it off. "Hey! He just sent me a photo!" She stared at it, hand over her heart, then passed me the phone.

It was a picture of Kyle in his camo fatigues, holding a pink flower toward the camera.

A Desert Rose for you.

I put an arm around her. "That's so beautiful. One month left?"

She sniffed. "One month left." She texted him quickly, then put away her phone. "Shall we dance?"

"Let's do this."

We replaced our high heels with sparkly flip-flops and hurried onto the dance floor. Iz and Rob were bumping and grinding like there was no tomorrow. Well, *she* was bumping and grinding, and *he* was loving every minute of it.

The music was solid, a mixture of dance and electronic, which was better than you'd expect at a school prom. Because of the cash-strapped committee, my classmate, Max, was spinning the tunes. He was a shy science wiz by day, but he moonlighted as DJ Maximus.

"I love this song!" Iz cried out and started doing worship

bows toward the DJ. We all joined in.

Then we were bouncing. Iz's dress was so low-cut that she had to hold herself in. The prom photographer, a junior named Ryan, hovered nearby snapping photos, poised for a wardrobe malfunction.

I was glad I'd come tonight. It was cool seeing everybody excited and dressed up. These last few months had been full of moments I wanted to forget and others I wanted to remember. I had a feeling that this moment, as we jumped up and down on the dance floor, was one to hang on to.

I felt a tug of yearning for Ortiz, but I reminded myself that I'd be with him soon. Forget the after-prom parties—I was going to Ortiz's place to snuggle with him until dawn.

When a slow song came on, Abby and I went to the punch table. One of the deans insisted on serving the punch himself, guarding it from spikers as if it were the Holy Grail.

I felt a tap on my shoulder. Abby was looking past me with a big smile.

"Wanna dance?" a male voice said behind me.

I turned around. "No way!"

Ortiz was standing there. He wore a white short-sleeved dress shirt, black tie slightly askew, and black jeans. His broken arm was in a sling. Any observer might say that with all his bruises and cuts, he looked like a dead prom king from a horror flick. But all I saw was the guy underneath, the one I loved so much it hurt. I hugged him, trying not to press on his injuries.

"I wanted to give you this." With his good hand, he slid a corsage over my wrist. "Should we dance?"

"Sure, but . . . we could sit instead."

"It's cool." He took my hand.

We went to the dance floor and wrapped our arms around each other. Iz and Rob shouted us out.

"You didn't have to do this," I said. "Must've hurt to stuff yourself into those clothes."

"It's no big deal. I'm just not sure I got the tie right."

I bit my lip against a laugh. "I think it looks cute."

"I'll take cute over sloppy any day." He smiled. "I figured if I didn't get to dance with you at your prom, I'd regret it. I want you to look back on your prom and remember me there." He said against my hair, "I want you to remember that I loved you way back then."

My heart melted. Tears rolled down my face, probably messing up my mascara. Oh well, we'd look like a dead prom king *and* queen, for all I cared.

He held me close, so close I could feel our hearts beating together. I asked myself the same question I'd been asking for weeks. How could I be so lucky to be loved by Ortiz?

I thought about what Julia had said—that nothing was random, that everything happened as it should. Maybe she was right. I wondered how I would've reacted six months ago if I'd been told that I'd be to hell and back, but would come out with the love of my life by my side. I hoped I would've said: *Bring it on.*

THE NEW

TOMORROW WAS THE BIG DAY. The day we moved to Tallahassee.

Tonight, Iz was hosting a huge end-of-summer party. Or, as she put it, *the party to end all end-of-summer parties.*

When I walked through the door, Iz hugged me and shoved a Maddie Diaz Margarita into my hand. "Where's your man?" she asked, glancing past me.

"He's having a drink with a coworker from Sasso's. He's coming later." I'd deliberately planned it that way, hoping to have some time with the girls before the party went full force. But judging by the crowd that had already arrived, I was too late.

A couple of girls from our school came in next. I said hello, then spotted Abby, who was sitting on her boyfriend's lap.

Kyle had come back a week ago and had no plans to deploy again anytime soon. But when he finally did, I had no doubt that Abby would continue to hold his spot for him. She'd hold it as long as she had to, until he was back for good.

Thankfully, Ortiz and I wouldn't have to be apart. We'd driven up to Tallahassee two weeks ago and found him an apartment, since I would be living in a dorm for my first year. We'd also checked out the Tallahassee Community College campus. He had enrolled in the criminal justice program, which would prepare him for the police academy. That was Ortiz; when he set his mind on something, he was unstoppable.

Carmen came up and hugged me. Soon after her prom, Rafael had dumped her for another girl. She was still ultra-emotional. It was as if all of her new confidence had left with him. Although Iz was encouraging her to hunt for a rebound, I hoped she wouldn't find one until she'd stabilized.

"All packed?" she asked.

I nodded. "The front hall is stacked with boxes. I have no idea if it's all going to fit in Ortiz's car."

"I'm surprised you guys aren't moving in together."

I shrugged. "I don't think Mom would go for that." But it wasn't just about my mom. Ortiz and I wanted to date. To be normal. Neither of us needed the pressure of moving in together right now.

I went out to the back porch to get some air. Everyone was talking about their plans. Some of them were leaving Miami; most of them were staying. But everyone had a direction. Even the directionless had chosen that as their direction.

I sipped my drink, absorbing the late summer air and looking out at the fading night sky. I found myself wishing I'd asked Ortiz to come a little earlier. My hand ached to be holding his.

"Diaz, you're pretty quiet."

I turned to see Manny standing there, hands in his pockets. I hadn't realized that Iz had invited him.

"That's me," I said. "The epitome of chill."

Something had changed between me and Manny since the night of Ortiz's kidnapping—the lightness between us was gone. We had never even talked about what had happened.

"You're moving tomorrow, and you're so laid back you're almost horizontal." Manny pulled up a chair and sat backward, resting his arms on the top. "Nothing ever fazes you, does it, Diaz?"

"*Everything* fazes me. But I deal." I'd meant to say it lightly, but it didn't come off that way.

"It was nice working with you, Diaz. Thanks for putting up with me." His smile turned serious. "You never blew me off, not even after you found out about my past."

"I know who you are," I said simply.

"There's something I have to get off my chest. Something I can't shake."

"No worries. I already figured out why you sent me down to the basement that night. It was to keep me safe."

"That's not what I meant." His eyes held mine. "I did what I had to do. I wouldn't change it."

"What, then?"

"Your man, Ortiz. I met his sister once."

"You did?"

He nodded. "The Reyes had her in this apartment. Place was a wreck. I saw her come out of the bedroom. I knew why she was there." He hung his head, and I wasn't sure if he would go on. "I was the newbie in the gang. I told myself that if I snitched, they'd know it was me. That's how I explained it away. Self-preservation."

I exhaled slowly. There was nothing I could say.

"Her eyes were so sad." Manny looked down at his hands. "Some days I can hardly live with it, you know? But I've got a way to make it right. Or at least, make things better."

"What do you mean?" I asked, afraid of the answer.

He lowered his voice to a whisper. "X told me what he and the Destinos are doing."

"But Salazar's dead."

"Yeah, but there are others like him. Always will be. I wanted you to know that . . . that I'm gonna help." Before I could begin to argue with him, he got up. "Keep in touch, okay?"

"Bet on it." My mind still whirled from everything he'd said, but I gave him a hug.

He started to walk away, then he turned around. "If he disappoints you, I'll be here. Don't forget that."

I nodded. "I won't forget." But I knew that Ortiz would never let me down.

By the time Ortiz showed up, the party was in overdrive. The walls and floors thumped. I was surprised that the cops hadn't shut us down, but knowing Iz, she'd gone over to her neighbors' earlier today with potted plants to soften them up.

It was too loud for talking, so we didn't. Ortiz's arm was around me, his hand settled in the curve of my waist. We watched Julia and Eric heat up the dance floor. They were a couple who, like us, had faced the fire—and had survived, stronger than ever.

More people came in. Iz cranked the music louder. She was all over the place, chatting, dancing, slinging drinks and spreading out food. It hit me that I missed her already—both those things I loved about her, and those things I didn't love. Iz would never, ever be boring.

As I watched my friends, I realized how much I was going

to miss them. Strange how I could feel sad and happy all at the same time.

— *Moving forward always means leaving something behind,* I thought. *I'll miss you all. But I'll be back.*

Ortiz said into my ear, "Our future starts now."

I looked up at him and smiled. He was right about that. Destiny was leading us in a new direction. And we were going there together.

ACKNOWLEDGMENTS

A big thanks to my editor, Kari Sutherland, for her warmth and insight. And to the incredible team at HarperTeen, including Jen Klonsky, Alice Jerman, and the art department for the amazing cover.

Thanks to John Rudolph, my agent. You are awesome.

Hugs and high fives to the Firkin writers.

Not least, my loving family. I'm so lucky to have you.

JOIN

THE COMMUNITY AT

Epic Reads
Your World. Your Books.

FIND
the latest books

DISCUSS
what's on your reading wish list

CREATE
your own book news and activities to share with friends

ACCESS
exclusive contests and videos

Don't miss out on any upcoming EPIC READS!

Visit the site and browse the categories to find out more.

www.epicreads.com

HARPER TEEN
An Imprint of HarperCollins Publishers